STRUAN

GUARDS OF CLAN ROSS

ISBN: 978-1-960608-02-4

ALSO BY HILDIE MCQUEEN

Guards of Clan Ross

Erik

Torac

Struan

Clan Ross of the Hebrides

The Lion: Darach

The Beast: Duncan

The Eagle: Stuart

The Fox: Caelan

The Stag: Artair

The Duke: Clan Ross Prequel

Clan Ross Series

A Heartless Laird

A Hardened Warrior

A Hellish Highlander

A Flawed Scotsman

A Fearless Rebel

A Fierce Archer

Moriag Series

Beauty and the Highlander

The Lass and the Laird

Lady and the Scot

The Laird's Daughter

CHAPTER ONE

Early Spring, Southeastern area of South Uist

THERE WASN'T MUCH archer Struan Maclean enjoyed more in life than pursuing and conquering an enemy. With a lithe body, wide shoulders, and impressive upper body strength, he was made for archery. On this day, however, every muscle in his body ached. The urge to stretch so intense, it had him clenching his jaw.

No matter his discomfort, Struan kept his vigil from high atop a tree, lodged between two thick branches, with his cloak as the only defense against the chilly spring breeze. Hidden in trees lining the path were several other archers, who all maintained the same constant vigil.

Over the last year, they'd fought against foreign aggressors who'd managed to slip in, plunder and kill, then retreat without being caught.

Despite Clan Ross warriors giving chase, it had been impossible to figure out where these attackers were coming and going from without a trace.

It wasn't until recently that Struan and Torac—a warrior and friend—had discovered the narrow passage to a cove that was hidden on two sides by hills.

Men were put on watch and had spotted boats the day before, which was why the archers were now on guard.

Vigilant guard.

Everyone was on edge. Certain the aggressors would soon be caught and finally dealt with before they could cause any further harm to the people of the Isle.

At the sign of movement, Struan signaled Caelan, the young archer closest to him, and Caelan signaled the other archer closest to him, and so on. Then they all directed their full attention to Struan, who notched an arrow onto his bow and lifted it into position, signaling the other archers to do the same.

This was a perfect assignment for archers, the attack would be fast and silent. Since the pirates had never brought archers to the previous attacks, Struan figured there was little danger to them.

First one, then a second, then a third man appeared below. They moved inland down the narrow path with caution. Moving silently, communicating with signals.

The first man stopped and scanned the area before signaling for them to continue forth. By the wariness of their leader, Struan knew the man had a sense something was wrong. But like most people who were covering familiar ground, they never thought to look up. Not that they could have seen Struan and his carefully concealed archers.

A fatal mistake, not to listen to that inner voice, Struan thought as he scanned the trees to meet each archer's gaze. They would wait until most of the intruders were in sight.

Finally, the line of men stretched almost to the opening of the narrow passage, one behind the other, as if lined up for target practice.

Struan nodded and arrows rained down.

At first, the men below seemed confused as their comrades fell. By the time they realized what was happening, it was too late. Many of the enemy dropped to the ground immediately lifeless. Those who didn't tried to crawl away, only to have several more arrows sink deep into their bodies.

It was gruesome and satisfying at the same time. It was the end to the terror caused by intruders who did not hesitate to kill innocent people. Once again the people of Clan Ross were safe from danger.

A few at the beginning of the passage who were not far in managed to escape and run back toward the shore. Struan lifted his bow, aimed, and hit one in the leg. The man screamed and fell forward, then managed to get up and hobble a bit more.

The second time Struan took aim, the man fell to the ground lifeless.

Those who hoped to escape, stopped at the appearance of the laird's birlinns surrounding the boat and effectively preventing any possibility of escape.

The battle—if one could call it that—was quickly over.

Ross warriors, who'd been just outside the narrow path, came into view, with swords drawn, and began the task of dispatching any who'd survived the assault of arrows.

The rope slid effortlessly past his leather-wrapped hands as Struan rappelled down from his perch. The other archers also lowered silently to the ground, with only a soft sound when their boots touched the ground.

"Patrol the area. Ensure no one escaped into the trees," Struan ordered his men and then stalked toward the boat, interested to find out any information about where the foreigners came from.

If the aggressors were organized, they could've given other pirates directions to the cove, and it meant Clan Ross guards would need to continue to patrol the area.

Caelan caught up to him. "Where are ye going?"

"To the boat. I want to hear what is said."

The cold seawater sloshed against their lower legs as they walked over to claim the dead men's rowboat. Struan rowed the boat to the larger vessel, and once reaching it, they used ropes to pull themselves up the side of the boat to the deck.

Ross warriors were already on board, searching every inch for any man who hid or any items of interest.

On the forward bow, several men knelt, their hands and ankles bound.

Gavin, the leader of the warriors assigned to the nearby village of Taernsby, walked up to one of the bound men. "Who is yer leader? Did he go with the others?" He pointed toward the shore.

The man spat at the warrior and remained silent.

Gavin motioned to the two who flanked the bound man. "Show the others what happens when they do nae talk."

The guards lifted the man, who began to struggle and dumped him over the side. There was a scream followed by a splash as the hapless man sunk to his death.

"Ye will nae get any answers from him now," Struan said.

The warrior's flat gaze met his. "Though the others may be more forthcoming."

"True," Struan said. As much as he hated the ways of battle, it was a necessary evil.

"Over here," Caelan called. Struan followed the younger

man through a doorway they had to stoop to fit through and into a cramped room.

On a surface were scribbled notes, all written in a different language. The map, however, he could read. They'd circled several locations on the isle, including the cove they were at now.

"Looks like they were the ones who also attacked the northern shore. The laird will be glad for this information."

Just then the laird's brother, Duncan Ross, entered. His huge size making the already cramped space feel airless. "What is it?"

Struan motioned to the map. "The answers to many questions."

Duncan nodded, the usually solemn man's face softening. "Finally."

Other than the map and some stolen items, they didn't find too much of interest. Struan and Duncan agreed that the laird's brother would take the map to the keep. Once the laird studied all the information, a decision would be made about further assignments.

"One of them speaks our language," a warrior, who'd been dealing with the prisoners, announced from the doorway. "We may want to keep him to read the notes and such."

"Aye," Duncan replied. "Keep him and the lad with them."

The warrior turned and ran back to the deck.

Struan and Caelan followed and watched as the lad was fished out of the water coughing and gasping for air.

The warrior looked over his shoulder at a frowning Duncan. "He spat at me."

Upon sensing he was safe, the boy sat up and glared at the

warrior. It was obvious to Struan the boy could turn out to be dangerous upon growing up.

"Ye should probably send him off on the boat with the old man to ensure they let their people know not to come here."

Duncan stared at the boy. "We will question them first, then possibly, send him away. He may grow up to return and seek revenge."

An older man sat huddled in the corner of the bow, his gaze moving between them and the boy. "Let him live. I will tell ye all ye wish to know."

THE GUARD POST, where Struan lived, was an hour's ride from the passage. And to get to the post, he would have to ride through the village of Taernsby.

Taernsby was a bustling village with several taverns, inns, bakeries, and butcher shops. There was always plenty of activity, which drew many to come there daily. There was a large market where it was easy to get inexpensive prepared food and upon his stomach growling, Struan decided it was what he'd do.

It was too late for the market stalls to be open, but he could find food at either the tavern or several houses where villagers sold food cooked in their own kitchens and served on tables outside the door.

A village widow was such a person, she had a table and benches outside of her front door where she offered goat stew and bread.

Struan dismounted and guided his horse to a post near the widow's house and tethered it. A man already sat eating and they greeted each other with a head bob as Struan lowered to sit on the opposite side of the sturdy square table.

Moments later, the older woman appeared and slid a bowl of steaming stew in front of him and a wrapped bundle next to it.

"Ale?" she asked without looking at him.

"Aye."

The aroma of the stew made his stomach grumble with appreciation, and he grabbed the chunk of bread that was in a wrapped cloth and used it to scoop the food into his mouth.

After eating, he handed the woman a coin and went to his horse.

Without meaning to, he glanced across the way to a tiny room attached to the bakery and wondered if the woman was there.

Weeks earlier, he'd been propositioned by a woman, who was much too beautiful to live alone. She'd been hungry and without any kind of skills to make a living. Instead of accepting her offer, he'd fed her, given her a couple coins, and advised her to find work.

It had been obvious, to him at least, that she'd never worked as a whore, or had any idea how terrible a life that could be.

Sooner or later, something would happen to the wee lass. He had no doubt about it. Someone would take notice of her beauty and then take advantage of the defenseless woman.

It was best to check on her. Nothing more. At least that is what he told himself as he walked away from the table, across the square, and stood at the door.

He'd come to the village several times before and had only spotted her once. She'd been sweeping the front steps to the church.

Struan knocked on the door.

After a long moment just as he was about to walk away, the door creaked open, just wide enough for her to peer out. Her eyebrows rose in surprise.

"Ye should nae open the door if not sure who it is. It would be easy for me to push it open," Struan said in a gruff voice.

Her eyes narrowed and she opened the door wider and cocked her head to the side, seeming to size him up. It was comical as she was so small. "How am I to know who is knocking? I can nae see through wood."

"A hole," Struan replied looking past her to note not much had changed since the day he'd met her. There was a cot to one side, with a chair next to it. There was also a washstand. A small table was an addition from the last time he'd seen her.

"What do ye want?" she asked looking over her shoulder. "I do not have coin to repay ye. Ye never brought me the tunics to mend."

"Have ye eaten?" Struan wasn't sure why he asked, but he did wish to know. Perhaps he felt a kinship with her since, like him, she had no one. She'd been abandoned after a shipwreck with no recourse for fending for herself, or anyone to go to.

"I have." She gave him a challenging look. "I am surviving."

Struan met her gaze. "I will bring the tunics." He took a step back. "Be with care."

Once again her gaze narrowed. "As if ye care."

"Ye should not open..." The door closed firmly, and he couldn't help but chuckle. The woman reminded him of himself. When at a young age, he'd had to fend for himself. It had been the worse time of his life, and a time of learning not to trust.

The woman had not quite learned the lesson. As he stood there looking at the closed door, he hoped hers would not be a hard one.

Struan shook his head. What did it matter. Life would do what came naturally and there wasn't anything anyone could do about it. It wasn't as if anything he did or said would make a difference. Besides, he was not responsible for her well-being.

Taking a step away, he stopped and turned back to look at the tiny home once more. Then again, she was his responsibility. As guard to the laird, he was, in fact, responsible for the safety of the clan's people.

Admittedly, something about the pretty lass tugged at him. But he told himself it was merely that they were sort of kindred spirits.

It was then he noticed a man sleeping next to his vegetable stand. He walked over, plucked a pair of carrots and left a coin.

His steed ate the offerings with greed, then drank deeply from a trough he led it too. Satisfied the horse was done drinking, Struan mounted the huge beast and continued to the guard post, where there would be discussions about all that had occurred and all that had been discovered in the interrogations of the men aboard the ship. And what, if anything, they had learned from the two they had allowed to live.

He doubted any of the men, who'd been left behind on the boat, knew much. One of the dead was probably the leader.

The guard house was large, with a huge room in the front where cots lined both sides. On the right between the cots was a massive hearth where a fire was kept burning to dispel cold. Straight forward in the rear area were several long tables, where the men took their meals. When the weather permitted, they ate at other tables outside.

To the left of the tables was a wide door that led to a well-stocked kitchen. The area was ruled by a woman named Alpena, and her two helpers. The women were older and good cooks. The food was always flavorful.

Behind the tables, to the right, was another doorway that lead to a few small bedchambers. One was occupied by Gavin, leader over all the guards. The second was used by Graeme, the healer. The third Struan shared with Quinn, who along with him fell in line beneath Gavin. Two other leaders had rooms as well.

As he approached the outside of the building, he was surprised to see his friend, Torac Bratton, who walked over to greet him.

Struan dismounted and smiled broadly. "What brings ye?" They embraced as brothers.

If he were to be honest, Torac and Erik Larsen, the leader of the men stationed at another village, had been like his family for the last ten years. The three of them had fought and patrolled together more times than he could count.

"Why are ye here?" Struan repeated, guiding his mount to the stables.

"Ye," Torac replied falling into step beside him. "I was on patrol, heard of the battle, and came to ensure ye were not injured."

"They were not expecting us, did not take any care. Clan Ross vanquished them easily and we had no injuries," Struan replied blandly, not wishing to let his friend know how good it felt that someone cared enough to come and see about him.

Torac grunted. "I am glad to hear it."

"Have ye not spoken to anyone yet?"

The warrior shook his head. "I have only just arrived."

Upon entering the guardhouse, Gavin stood by the tables in the back of the room. He spoke loudly, his voice resonating over the silent men.

"An older man, who claimed to be the cook, said there were more boats. He and a young lad were allowed to live. They are here in the room to the side, locked in. We will question them further in the morning."

"What of the boat?" Struan asked.

"It will be moved to another shoreline, to be used as a decoy."

"Doubtful it will work. They will suspect something is wrong," Torac remarked.

Gavin nodded. "I think so as well. However, it may also work as a deterrent."

Patrol assignments were given to the warriors. Gavin instructed Struan to do the same with the archers.

"Come over here," Struan called out to his men and signaled for them to meet him just outside the door. The archers waited impatiently for him to speak. Most of them exhausted after spending so many hours in the trees.

"We will allow the warriors to conduct most of the patrols. However, we will help with lookouts closer to the shoreline. Tomorrow we will begin to build a platform between trees from where we can take turns guarding."

The men grumbled at the thought of spending time up in a

tree for hours on end. Struan didn't blame them. "It is either that or ye can hang from a branch like a squirrel, it's up to ye."

They silenced.

"Tomorrow rest. The day after we practice, and assignments will be given. I will go to the village to find someone who can build the platforms. I do nae trust my life with something ye lot put together."

The men laughed, looking to one another in agreement.

A BONFIRE HAD been started and he and Torac walked to it. They lowered to sit on benches that had been placed there by whoever built the fire.

"Do ye like it here?" Torac asked. "Ye seem to have things well in hand."

Struan gave a one shoulder shrug. "Where I work is no matter. As long as I serve the laird and have food in my belly, I am well."

His friend studied him for a long moment. Instinctively Struan knew the man had something to say.

"What is it?"

"Leana is with child," Torac said, his face taut. "I am not sure how I feel about it."

Of the three of them—Erik, Torac, and Struan—Torac had always been the levelheaded one. The one whom he'd often gone to for advice. It was strange that the man seemed to want advice from him now.

"A bairn. That is uncharted territory my friend. Women seem to instinctively know what to do. I am sure Leana will order ye about to ensure ye do what needs to be done."

His friend nodded, a slight lifting to the corners of his lips.

"Many women die giving birth."

"Aye, true," Struan said, not mincing words. "Many do, but yer wife is strong stock is she not?"

Torac's gaze bore into his as if seeking to see the future, and he let out a breath. "Yer words make me feel better."

"Aye well, ye have nothing to worry about. How is Erik?"

They talked for a while, the entire time Struan grateful for Torac's visit. He did miss the conversations that came so naturally between them.

"What about ye? A lass ye have an eye on?"

At the question, a picture of the slight woman, whose name he'd not bothered to ask formed in his mind and Struan frowned. Large blue eyes, looking up at him with a trust he didn't deserve. The way her midnight black hair framed her face, the light pinkening of her cheeks when he'd admonished her for opening the door. She was worthy of being admired.

"So there is," Torac said with a chuckle.

"There is nae," Struan snapped. "I was considering who to speak to about building the platform tomorrow morning."

"Mmm," Torac replied, a teasing arch of a brow. "I will go with ye. Then I must continue back to Welland."

CHAPTER TWO

Lingering in her cot was the best way to stay warm. There was no hearth in Grace Durie's tiny room and curled up in a ball under several blankets was the only way to stop from shivering. Soon she would have to rise, and it was something she rarely looked forward to.

Every day was a repeat of the one before. A struggle to find a way to survive to the next.

Thankfully, she'd acquired work cleaning the vicarage every other day, which didn't pay much, but she was offered a daily meal with the vicar and his wife. And most days it was her only meal.

Cleaning and sweeping around the vicarage was light work, probably given to her out of pity, but Grace was thankful for it. She could survive on one meal a day. And with the coin she earned weekly, she could save up and purchase necessities.

Today, she'd speak to the seamstress and offer to work without pay. It would give her the opportunity to learn a skill.

Pushing the blankets away, she studied her limited clothing options. Upon coming ashore after the shipwreck, Grace was able to salvage only one trunk. Probably because no one was interested in the pitiful belongings that she'd brought with her.

Three frocks, stockings, a chemise, and several kerchiefs. Her other trunk with a pair of new dresses, some shoes, scarves, and a few pieces of jewelry was not found. It was also possible it was found and taken.

Pushing the thoughts aside, she relieved herself in the chamber pot she kept under the cot and then washed up with water she'd gotten from the well the day before.

Once she donned one of her frocks, a brown one, she braided her hair and tied a kerchief over it. She hoped to look dowdy and uninteresting. The less attention she garnered from men, the better.

After discarding the contents of the chamber pot and rinsing it, she placed it back under the cot and straightened the blankets.

The thought of leaving her cozy home made her shiver. It wasn't that she feared anything in particular, it was that each time she walked outside, the stark reminder of having no one to care about her or keep her safe brought a heavy sadness over her.

Grace took a tiny bundle of coins, unbuttoned her blouse, and tucked it between her breasts. She had no other place to hide them and was too afraid to leave the pitiful amount she'd saved there.

At the snug bundle against her breast, she thought of the warrior who'd given her a pair of coins and had come to see about her the night before. He had yet to bring the tunics and although she wanted to pay him back, it was interesting that he'd not taken advantage of the one and only time she'd been desperate enough to offer her body in exchange for coin.

It had been a pitiful attempt, but after not eating for several days, she'd been barely able to stand.

Although large in size, muscular, and with a constant stern expression, the warrior inspired trust. Instinctually, Grace knew he wouldn't harm her. Instead of taking advantage of her, he'd fed her and given her a few coins.

There was something in his dark green gaze that made Grace forget about the dreariness of her life. His stern intimidating presence was like a wall of protection when he was about. Though he seemed to be a man of honor, Grace remained vigilant, careful.

The past was a good teacher of what happened when one put too much trust in others.

Closing the door firmly behind, Grace walked across the street, turned right, and then hurried down another until arriving at the village center.

The market was open, people calling out and offering their wares.

Her stomach growled, but she did not give in to the tempting offers of sizzling meats and fresh bread aroma wafting in her direction.

Instead, she walked around to where the seamstress had her shop.

When she opened the door and walked in, the atmosphere inside was inviting. There were bolts of fabric strewn about, seemingly not in any order, but to Grace it was obvious there was a purpose for where each was. One stack of coordinating colors would make a gown, while the other of dark thick ones were to be sewn into tunics.

"I do not believe to have met ye, but I have spotted ye on occasion," a pretty woman of about thirty said walking into the room. "Do ye wish for a new dress?" The woman walked closer and took Grace in.

"I may have one already made."

She stopped and giggled, the laughter making her seem much younger. "I should allow ye to talk. Working alone makes me glad for company." Her sparkling brown eyes met Grace's. "I am Flora."

"Grace," she replied. "I am not here to have a dress made. I have no coin. I wish to offer to work, without pay. I need to learn a trade."

Flora nodded, her brows coming together in thought. "Let us discuss this proposition of yers while we eat." She waved to the back of the space. "There is a table back here."

They settled into chairs and Flora poured a hot cider into two cups. She then took a loaf of bread and tore it into two large chunks. Atop the bread, she placed thinly cut meat and handed one to Grace.

It was difficult for her not to gobble the offering, but she managed to eat with a bit of decorum.

"Where do ye come from?" Flora asked between bites.

"The shipwreck," Grace replied. "I live two streets over in the room next to the other bakery. The proprietors allow me to live there in exchange for my sweeping the floors, for which I am grateful."

The woman pushed back an errant strand of red hair and let out a long sigh. "Did ye lose anyone aboard the ship?"

"I was betrothed," Grace replied. "He never came to collect me. I have no one other than myself now."

There was a sadness in Flora's expression that almost made Grace cry. The woman stopped eating and gazed toward the front windows. "I too came to be here after a shipwreck. I lost my husband and bairn. For many months I wished to have died with them." Her moist eyes slid to Grace. "I am glad ye did not lose anyone that way."

"That is horrible." Grace touched Flora's arm feeling bad for the woman. Although she'd heard the other shipwreck had taken place years earlier, it was obvious the pain remained just as fresh in Flora's mind.

"Ye can work here," Flora announced abruptly. "I do need help. The other woman who worked here, recently left. She and her husband moved to be closer to her mother and father."

Grace's face brightened, but then she looked down at the table. "I have only mended clothes, I know little more than that."

"Ye can begin with hems and such. I will teach ye anything else ye may need."

They continued to eat, Grace's stomach settling at knowing she was making headway and would hopefully soon be able to afford a home with a small hearth.

"I know the room ye live in," Flora said. "The old man who used to live there was a nasty sort. How did ye find it?"

At recalling the dismal filthy room, Grace couldn't stop the shudder. "Filthy. It took me days to clean it. I could not stand to sleep there, so I slept on the floor in the bakery."

"Burt is good to allow people to live there without paying. He and his wife are compassionate people."

Grace nodded. "I am so very grateful for them. At the end of each day, I clean up the bakery to repay their kindness."

"Ye work at the vicarage as well," Flora said surprising her.

"They are kind as well."

"Aye," Grace replied.

Flora's expression turned serious. "There are many who are not as kind or compassionate. Ye have been fortunate. Do be with care."

They came to an agreement that Grace would come there in the mornings on the days she did not work at the vicarage. Then in the afternoons after she finished at the vicarage.

The seamstress would place her work on a small table where Grace would hem gowns and tunics. Flora insisted she be paid, and the amount made Grace very happy.

As she settled into the small table her heart swelled with gratefulness. The next day when she went to the vicarage, she planned to pray and thank God for her blessings.

Flora was kind and genuine and immediately they fell into a good work rapport, often staying later, to talk and share about each other's lives.

"Would ye go to the market and purchase items for supper? Ye will join me for last meal of course," Flora said handing Grace a basket and a couple of shillings. She rattled off a list as she cut beautiful blue fabric for a gown.

THE MARKET WAS bustling as women came out to shop for that evening's supper. Grace weaved between stalls scanning the offerings. She would buy the best items for their meal to ensure Flora was pleased.

An elderly couple displayed plush cabbages and fat carrots and she hurried over. She'd enough to buy one of the two and then meat from the butcher. Closing the distance, she waited as a woman bartered for a lot of cabbages, onions, and apples.

Grace wondered how many people she was to feed.

They came to an agreement and the woman motioned to another one and they began placing the items into a pair of baskets.

"Do ye require help, Alpena?" The deep voice made Grace whirl and find herself against a wall of muscle and leather. The green gaze lowered to hers when she looked up.

It was him, the man who'd fed her once.

"Pardon me," she said stepping sideways.

"Ah, nay, Struan," the woman, Alpena, said waving him away. "Go see about what ye came for. I have a pair of lads who will take all of this to the wagon."

Grace didn't move, unsure of what to do, she remained frozen. The man turned to her. "How fare ye?"

Grace swallowed, her throat dry. The reaction a repeat of each time she'd seen him. Her heartbeat quickened and her palms became moist. It was ridiculous. She cleared her throat.

"I am well." Grace tried to push past him to the stall, but he didn't budge.

"Have ye eaten?"

The same question he'd asked each time they met. Why did he care so much?

"Aye, I have. With Flora, the seamstress."

Without expression he looked her over, then scrutinized the basket in her hands. "Are ye to purchase food?"

"Flora gave me coin to acquire items for supper." Her voice broke a bit at thinking that perhaps she should just hand him the bundle from between her breasts. She still had one of the three silver coins he'd given her. "I am saving to repay ye."

"No need to repay me. It was a gift. I brought the tunics.

Can I bring them to yer home?"

Surprised and glad at the same time, she shook her head. "I will be at Flora's all day. Ye can bring them there."

He nodded and walked away without another word.

"*Struan*," Grace whispered. The strong name suited him.

IT WAS COZY and warm inside the seamstress shop when she returned. Her pulse had yet to settle since seeing Struan and learning his name.

Each time the front door opened Grace's gaze flew to it expecting he'd enter and bring his sewing.

Several hours had passed and Struan had yet to deliver the tunics for her to mend. A part of her wished he would not have told her, it was maddening to be so distracted when doing her best to sew a perfectly straight line with even stitches.

A moment later when the door opened, it was a woman who entered, with a younger girl in tow.

"Flora, I require yer help," the woman said in a haughty tone, her narrowed eyes scanning the space.

"What can I do?" Flora asked getting to her feet immediately and going to where the woman waited.

Something about the woman made Grace take an instant dislike to her. With the expression of someone who is constantly bothered, she had an unfriendly demeanor.

Instead of replying to Flora, the woman once again scanned the room until her gaze rested on Grace. "Are ye the one who lives by the bakery?"

"I am," Grace replied and continued to work on the hem she'd almost completed and did not wish to be distracted from.

"I am told ye are alone, without a husband."

Since it was a statement and not a question, Grace did not reply. The woman huffed. "Well?"

"Did ye ask me something?" Grace asked, finally looking up. Purposefully, she looked past the woman to Flora who rolled her eyes.

"I wondered how ye made coin, but I suppose *now*, ye do this." The woman accentuated the word *now* as if to make a point.

Before Grace could say anything, she turned to Flora. "I need this gown hemmed immediately. It is for a gathering at the constable's home this very evening."

Flora shook her head and then looked over her shoulder to the pile of work. "I cannot possibly. Not by tonight. It is already late in the day."

The woman let out a long breath. "I will pay ye extra." She looked to Grace. "What about ye, are ye able to do it?"

Grace's first instinct was to say no, but she considered how much she needed the coin. At the same time, her instinct told her to keep from it. "I am just learning. I would hate to ruin such a fine gown."

The woman whirled back to Flora. "After all this time paying ye well, how can ye not put me ahead of others?" Her shrill voice seemed to bounce off the walls.

"I will do it." Flora reached for the gown and took it. "I will send it to ye once it's completed."

"Do I not need to put it on for ye to pin?" the woman snapped.

"Of course," Flora said flustered, her cheeks pinkening

with annoyance.

While the woman changed, the young girl walked closer to where Grace sat. Her angelic face transformed into a sneer, and she whispered, "Mother says ye spend time with men in exchange for food. She said ye were in the tavern with a man. She said ye are a whore."

Her mother walked out. "Come here, Lily."

Grace could not do more than gape as the girl strolled to where Flora pinned the woman's gown. "Mother, I wish to leave now."

"One moment darling," the woman replied. "She is almost done."

"I do not care for how it smells in here," the girl continued sliding a look to Grace. "Ye said I should not be seen around her."

The woman gave the girl a pointed look. "No one is in here but us."

This time when the woman went to the back to get out of the pinned gown, the girl stood near Flora stealing curious glances at Grace.

When the woman came out from changing back into the outfit she'd walked in wearing, the front door opened, and Struan walked in holding a stack of tunics.

Immediately Grace's breath caught at seeing him. The warrior's presence shrunk the space, with his windblown hair and chiseled face set. His green gaze swept the room not hesitating until finding her in the back corner.

The woman and her daughter exchanged looks and then the mother blocked Struan from walking to where Grace sat. "I have not met ye but hear ye are close to our laird. Ye have a place of honor in the clan as a leader."

"Ye know more about me than I about ye," Struan replied, his voice curt.

"I am Marianna MacBain, my husband, Harold, is a prominent member of the village council. We have lived in Taernsby all our life."

Struan nodded. "Aye, I know Harold. He is a good man." He left the sentence hanging. "Pardon me." He took a step to the side when the woman placed her hand on his forearm.

"Are ye to attend the event tonight at the constable's home?"

Struan nodded. "All the leaders of the guard will be there."

"We must speak more," the woman said finally removing her hand. With that, she swept from the shop and just before closing the door turned to Flora. "Ensure the gown is delivered promptly."

"Of course," Flora replied and flattened her lips into a tight line. She turned to Grace. "I suppose I best start, before she has me drawn and quartered."

Grace pressed her lips together to keep from laughing.

"It is nice to see ye Struan," Flora said.

"Ye as well," he replied and slid a look to Grace. "I brought the mending."

Again her heart quickened, and butterflies took flight. If only there was a way to control her reaction to him. As her cheeks heated, she wondered if the others noticed the pinkening.

When he walked closer and placed the clothing on a side table, the scent of the outdoors filled her nostrils. His large body bent, and he studied the cloth in her hands, it was as if he were truly interested.

"Flora has been kind to teach me to hem properly. I do not need instruction to mend any tears or holes in yer tunics. I promise to do my best." Grace's voice trembled slightly, and she hoped he didn't notice.

This time his gaze moved from her hands to her lips and then her eyes. "It matters not, they are old."

"I have an idea," Flora called out. "Struan, would ye be willing to allow Grace to learn to make a tunic using ye to measure? Ye do require new tunics." Her gaze swept over the worn one he wore.

A gasp escaped Grace and she looked anywhere but to Struan. If he said no, it would be hurtful. But if he said yes, she would surely be unable to learn a single thing. He was much too distracting.

When he chuckled, it was a rich deep sound that Grace felt down to her bones. Was there anything about the man that did not affect her so?

"Aye, I will do it. I do require new clothes," he replied, and Grace sneaked a look at him. There was no expression on his face. "Though, I cannot today."

"That's fine. We do not have time today, perhaps in a pair of days?" Flora replied. "Whenever ye have some free time, return so Grace's lessons can begin."

"I will." He hesitated, glanced at Grace before walking out.

"Why did ye do that?" Grace exclaimed when the door closed. "The man makes me so nervous."

"Because he likes ye and ye are affected by him as well." Flora grinned. "I think it is charming."

"Goodness." It was all Grace could say as she watched out

the window to Struan's retreating form.

"Ouch." She'd pricked her finger.

Flora chuckled.

CHAPTER THREE

"**I** CONSIDERED INVITING Flora to attend with me, but she is too busy," Gavin, the leader of the guard told Struan as they rode behind the carriage carrying some of the guard's wives.

"Why would ye wish to bring her?" Struan replied. "Ye keep insisting she nothing more than a friend. That nothing romantic happens between ye."

Gavin gave him a droll look. "So she can have an enjoyable evening. The lass deserves it."

His mind instantly went to the wee lass Grace. Although she strived to be guarded, her expressive face told of her thoughts. It was curious how strong she was in the face of adversity and how well she carried herself. There was no doubt in his mind that Grace was a survivor.

"I did not think of that," he replied honestly, wishing he'd invited Grace to attend. It could be something she would have enjoyed. Then again, what did he know of her?

Gavin met his gaze and Struan realized he'd not responded to whatever the man had asked. He nodded and thankfully, it seemed to appease him.

"There will be plenty of ale and good food, which is enough for me. The laird wishes us to be present and ensure the village council and constable feel his presence," Gavin continued.

He studied the man who was almost as tall as him with thick black hair and an olive complexation. Although he'd liked Gavin upon meeting him, recognizing the air of authority about him, Struan had yet to figure out Gavin's way of thinking. One moment he was open, sharing his life and thoughts on things, the next he was so guarded, it was as if a thick wall materialized out of thin air.

Ahead the sounds of music and conversation drew them to the village hall. The building had been constructed just a year earlier to allow for gatherings during inclement weather that seemed to plague the Isle of Uist.

During the middle of winter, those who wished to sell their homemade goods were allowed to set up in the hall. Other times, celebrations were held there.

This time, it was obvious only certain people were invited, by the men posted at each door either allowing passage or sending people away.

He and Gavin must've been among the last to arrive given the fact that the men at the door were more interested in their tankards of ale, barely sparing them a glance as they dismounted and entered.

The room felt stuffy with so many people milling about behind closed doors. Tables were laden with trays of meat, while those hired to serve walked around offering ale to anyone whose cup ran low.

He was immediately offered a tankard and gladly took it, taking a long draw. He walked to where other guards sat and lowered onto the bench.

The tray of meat was pushed in his direction and Struan

grabbed a piece. The air was festive with musicians playing lively tunes that filled the air intermingling with the conversations by those in attendance.

All he had to do was eat his fill, ensure his presence was noted before slipping out and going to the room he'd rented at the inn for the night.

It was later as he made his way back inside after relieving himself that he was accosted by the same woman from the seamstress shop.

"There ye are, I thought perhaps ye had not come. My husband wishes to speak to ye." A shiver of apprehension went up his spine as he crossed the room to where Harold McBain sat with several men.

The man stopped midsentence of whatever tale he told to look up at Struan and his wife nearing. "There ye are. Please join me."

With no choice, Struan lowered to the seat noting an exchange of looks between Harold and his wife. The man was obviously being steered by his wife to do something.

Harold was a loud boisterous storyteller that had everyone laughing. Even Struan could not help but enjoy the man's tales. He was well-liked by the fact others soon came closer to speak to him or hear whatever he spoke about.

With reddish hair, the jolly man had a thick matching beard and bright blue eyes. He turned to Struan. "I have been directed by my wife to speak to ye about a courtship between ye and my daughter, Lily. It seems the lass had taken notice of ye and is most persistent to get to know ye."

Not wishing to insult the man, Struan opted to pretend ignorance although he remembered the imp-looking blond lass. "Yer approval is most kind. However, I do not ever plan to marry."

"Ye remain young. My lass is a beauty and—"

Struan interrupted. "At thirty and two, I am much too old to marry someone who must not be more than fifteen summers."

"Lily is quite mature for her age. It is time for her to seek a husband."

That men looked to marry off their young daughters was something Struan didn't understand. The lass he'd seen at the seamstress's shop looked more like a child than a woman. He did not find her as someone desirable, but more someone who needed guidance and protection.

"I am flattered that ye find me worthy and hope ye do not take offense, but I must decline the offer of yer beautiful daughter."

The man stared at him as if in disbelief, then chuckled. "Ye must have yer eye on someone already." He then threw his head back and laughed. Holding up his tankard he shouted, "To desire without bounds!"

Others joined in adding spicier innuendos, thankfully taking Harold's attention and Struan was able to excuse himself and return to where the guards sat.

"What was that about?" Gavin asked leaning closer so that Struan could hear. "Did Harold have a request?"

"That I court his daughter," Struan replied with a grimace. "The lass is but fifteen summers and looks younger."

Gavin gave an exaggerated shudder. "I hope ye said no without insulting him."

"I do not think he was offended. I stated that I do not plan to marry, adding that I was much too old for his daughter."

Gavin seemed to mull over Struan's words. "He seems in good spirits. However, the wife is looking over as if trying to read our lips."

"I should have brought Grace." The image of the beauty, with dark tresses framing her face, the way her bright blue gaze seemed to follow his every move, and how her cheeks pinkened whenever he came near formed in his mind. But as soon as the words left his mouth, he wished to take them back. Why had he blurted such a thing?

"What I mean is a woman's presence keeps matchmaking parents away."

"Who is Grace?" Gavin asked.

"She is someone who survived the last shipwreck," Struan replied not adding any details. Not how he knew her, how they'd met, and certainly not that he'd bought her a meal at the tavern.

"Ah, yes, I know of whom ye speak," Gavin said. "Flora hired her to help. The wee lass is a beauty. I heard one of the guards plans to court her."

"Who?" The word flew from his lips.

With a grin, Gavin shrugged. "Quinn, for one."

Quinn was a huge man, who fought with a battle ax. Despite being a vicious warrior, Quinn was a fair man. Of all the warriors, he would be the one most would want at their back during battle.

Struan automatically looked for the man, only to realize that although a leader of a group of warriors, Quinn would never attend the type of gathering where he was expected to act a certain way.

Wild as a beast of the forest, Quinn had stated, he'd rather impale himself on a sword than prance about at a gathering.

It was hard to picture the huge man with such a wee lass. The thought made him annoyed for no particular reason, except that he felt protective of her. Of course, it was no more than his duty. Looking after the welfare of the people of Taernsby was his work. Nothing more.

"I need fresh air," Struan said and walked toward the entrance, only to be stopped by the constable.

Malcolm Pherson was a good and fair leader, well-liked by the townspeople, and held in high esteem by the laird.

"I require yer help," the man stated. "I spoke to Gavin, and he told me ye would be willing to escort some people to the keep, as ye planned to go there."

"Aye, I can do it. I have to be there in three days' time," Struan replied. He was looking forward to going to Duin Láidir and spending time at the keep. A perfect excuse to be away from Harold and his wife and their attempts to get him to court their daughter.

"Good," the constable replied with a smile. "I will ensure the two parties are aware."

"Who are they?" Struan asked, prepared to learn he'd be escorting a wagon filled with people hoping to have time with Laird Ross.

"A husband and wife who are asking for help in locating their son who's gone missing, and a wee lass who was aboard a ship that crashed into rocks near here. She is hoping to find out what happened to her betrothed."

It had to be Grace. Struan let out a breath and nodded. "Very well. I will meet them at the village square, early morn, three days hence."

He continued to the door, hoping the fresh air would help him decide what to do. On one hand, it was his turn to go to the keep, but he really did not wish to spend such a prolonged time alone with Grace.

All he had to do was to mention that Grace required escort to Quinn and the man would jump at the opportunity. Instantly Struan's shoulders lifted, and his neck tensed.

The cool breeze carried the sounds of the music and low din of conversation out to him, tingles of laughter filling the air.

Struan turned around at the sound of women's laughter. It was not coming from inside, but outside the hall. Walking around the side, he peered past a tall bush to see two women dancing. It was Flora and Grace. They held hands and turned in a circle in pace with the music inside.

"Our gathering is much better. We have fresh air and the company of stars," Flora exclaimed.

Grace released her friend's hands and performed a jig, her feet making quick work as she pranced from one foot to the other. "And we do not have to worry about anyone stepping on our toes."

Falling from its pins, part of her hair hung down past her shoulders, the silken cascade taking all his attention.

Flora laughed when Grace held her arms over her head and completed a perfect circle on her toes. "Ye are a graceful dancer."

"I used to dance all the time with my..." Grace stopped and let out a sigh. "Never mind."

Her betrothed was who she was about to say, Struan was

sure.

Feeling intrusive he turned to leave when a deep voice sounded. "Ladies. How fare ye?"

It was Quinn. The bulking man walked closer, ensuring to stop at a safe distance.

"Quinn," Flora greeted him in a friendly tone. "It is good to see ye." She introduced him to Grace, who became instantly reserved. Unlike just a moment earlier, she held her hands together in front of her and took a step back.

"Quinn is one of the laird's guards," Flora explained. "As a matter of fact, ye may be who will escort—"

"Has the celebration moved outside?" Struan interrupted, hoping Flora did not continue speaking.

The three looked to him. Struan was glad to see Grace relax somewhat at his presence. "Much nicer out here. Inside the air is still," Struan told them.

"They may have better food inside," Flora said with a wistful tone.

"I would not know," Quinn said. "I do not care for gatherings."

"Do ye?" Grace asked Struan, her gaze locking with his. "Enjoy gatherings?"

It was interesting because if anyone else would have asked, he would have instantly said no. In this instance, he realized that if escorting someone who obviously enjoyed music and celebration, he could see himself enjoying a gathering. The fact that she'd asked him directly made Struan's body react. His pulse quickened.

"I do, at times," he replied cautiously. "Ye?"

"Aye," she replied stealing a look to Quinn and Flora.

"What is not to like? People coming together to celebrate something. Everyone in good spirits."

There was an awkward silence and Struan looked to Quinn. "Are ye returning to the guard's quarters or remaining here in the village?"

"I was at the tavern and am heading back," Quinn replied.

"I will walk with ye to the horses. There is something I must speak to ye about," Struan wasn't sure what he'd tell the man, but he wished to take him away from being near Grace.

He looked to Flora and then met Grace's gaze. Flushed from dancing, she was even more beautiful than usual. Her black hair reflected the moonlight as her eyes slipped to his lips just long enough for him to notice. He didn't think anyone else did.

Quinn nodded in farewell, he attempted to hold Grace's gaze, but she instantly lowered her eyes. Struan felt a flicker of gladness. It was ridiculous. He had no desire to court her, or to be in any kind of relationship for that matter. Thus far in life he'd managed to be without complications and that was the best way to live, in his opinion.

He wanted to protect Grace. Nothing more.

AFTER MAKING UP some nonsense about how he required Quinn to help with leadership of the archers in his absence, he explained he was to go to the keep in three days.

"Are ye not returning to the guard's quarters?" Quinn asked.

"Aye, I will go and gather some clothes on the morrow, but I wished to speak to ye in case ye were gone out on patrol and I did not get the opportunity."

The man shrugged, not seeming to think it strange that Struan would ask something of him that would normally fall to Gavin.

The village square was quiet. It was late at night and those not at the gathering were probably abed.

At the sound of women's voices, he remained outside the inn, leaning on the building.

Flora and Grace walked arm-in-arm. They stopped in front of Grace's small home, and she walked inside. Flora continued to her shop, turning down a side street.

Unsure what possessed him, Struan cross the square and went to her door. He knocked softly so as not to scare her.

The door flew open. "Flora did ye…" Grace's eyes flew wide. "I thought ye was Flora."

"I have told ye not to open the door. At least ask first who it is." Struan admonished then feeling bad when her face fell.

"'Tis true. I am quite careless."

"Do not fret." Struan placed his hand on her shoulder, then removed it quickly. "The constable informed me that I am to escort ye and another pair to the keep."

She started. "Oh."

"We leave three days hence, early. I will meet ye in the square."

Grace nodded and looked up to meet his gaze. "I wish to ask about my betrothed. It is my duty is it not? Perhaps something happened and he is hurt. Besides, am I to remain alone?"

"I am sure the laird will try to help. Ye may never know what occurred as not everything is reported. But ye are not alone, ye have Flora…" He stopped short of adding…*and me.*

At the sight of tears trickling down her face, Struan's entire being wanted to stop them.

"Do not cry."

Grace sniffed. "To be alone without anyone who cares is so overwhelming at times."

He was shocked when she leaned forward, her face pushed against his chest as she cried. "I feel so very alone."

The passing of time had not eased her grief of how her family had sent her away. Perhaps it was the not knowing about her betrothed that didn't help matters. Struan could not imagine what she'd been through, seeing people drown. The last moments of so many lives lost.

"I am sorry," he said and wrapped her in his arms, allowing her grief to pour into him. "I will help ye find him. I promise."

At the words, she lifted her tear-streaked face up to him. "I am sorry. I am crying all over ye."

He didn't loosen his hold on her. Grace felt good against him. It was as if their bodies were familiar with one another's. When she sighed and leaned against him as if without any strength to stand on her own, Struan allowed it.

It was possibly the first time someone had held her while she cried, and Struan was glad to have the sad honor.

"Ye should rest," he finally said not wishing any revelers leaving the festivities to see them in an embrace and misconstrue things.

"I am sorry," she said again, finally moving away and wiping her face. "Thank ye."

Of its own and without any prompting, his body took over. Struan cupped her face and held it up to him. "Ye are admirable. A strong woman."

Then he kissed her. The press of his lips over hers was like nothing he'd ever experienced. Although he'd had relations with women before this night, he was not bothered by being celibate.

This time, however, it was different. So natural. And the awakening of his body was overwhelming.

They broke apart, both wordless and breathing rapidly past parted lips.

"I should not have done that," Struan said. "I bid ye a good night." He whirled around, quickly putting as much distance between them as he could. Because if he didn't, Struan was sure he would lift her in his arms and spend the night holding her.

"God's blood," he cursed. "Whatever is the matter with me?"

CHAPTER FOUR

A FTER A LONG time leaning against the door, Grace was finally able to will her legs to move. It was as if she floated to her cot and lowered to sit on it.

Not once since meeting her betrothed a year earlier when he'd visited her father, had she ever kissed a man.

Gilbert Duncan was an older, reserved man, whom she'd met but once. He'd kissed her upon informing her they were betrothed. It had been but a press of his lips atop hers, neither pleasant nor unpleasant, however, Grace had not liked it.

Although she'd not been attracted to him, the thought of leaving the horrible existence of her homelife was alluring.

Apparently, Gilbert asked her father for Grace, and he'd accepted. No one informed her until the following week, and even then, none of her questions were answered.

A pair of months later, the day before departing Grace was informed she would be sailing to South Uist in the Hebrides, from her home on the coast of mainland Scotland to meet with her betrothed.

There were no farewells, and barely any acknowledgement of her leaving the only life she'd ever known. When Grace had begun crying, instead of giving comfort, her stepmother had snapped that she ought to be thankful.

The night before leaving, she overheard her father and

stepmother talking. It seemed Gilbert Duncan had offered to pay off a large debt in exchange for her. They'd sold her to him.

Despite surviving, it was not sustainable. Grace had no doubt, her simple existence would be altered if anyone took notice of the fact she was alone without protection. More than anything, Grace wished for a husband and family. To be part of something. There had to be a good reason why Gilbert had not appeared to collect her. He'd paid a lot of money for her father to allow the marriage.

Grace let out a sigh. Struan had turned her mind into a jumbled mess. It was only since meeting him that she'd decided it was best to find her betrothed. The comment by the lass, Lily, had made up her mind.

It was not safe to remain alone without any kind of protection in the world she lived in. Despite kind people, like Flora, Grace knew it was only a matter of time before someone took advantage of her situation. Especially if the rumor spread of her being a whore.

Although Struan had kissed her, she did not think he'd planned to do so. He'd looked as shocked by his actions as she'd been. It had been an impulsive act of two people who were attracted to one another. But nothing of importance.

Her lips curved. It was almost as if he was scared of her. At the thought of such a strong man fearing her effect on him, Grace's spirits lifted.

THE NEXT DAY, upon arriving at the seamstress shop, Flora waved her in. "Lock the door and draw the curtains. I cannot risk any more work. I am so far behind."

Grace closed the door and drew the curtains shut. The room plunged into darkness. "We will have to leave the curtains open to allow us to see." Grace laughed and pulled them back open. "We can still keep the door barred."

Once again the room was light, and she went to the back table where there was bread and some cheese. "Ye went to the market early."

"Nay," Flora replied. "Gavin brought it early this morning."

Grace looked up from taking a bite. "He cares deeply for ye. Why does he not court ye?"

Her friend's cheeks pinkened. "He and I have a good friendship. I am not sure if we can move from that into something deeper. I am scared to lose him over it. I prefer things the way they are."

"Are ye not lonely?"

At the question, Flora gave her a knowing look. "I am not. I was married, had a good husband and a beautiful son and there is nothing that will ever replace it. I am happy."

"Good," Grace replied. "I am going to see the laird in a pair of days. I wish to ask about my betrothed."

By her expression, Flora was shocked. "Ye said he bought ye. Why would ye wish to be with a man ye are not attracted to? Surely, ye are not that lonely."

Although Flora meant well, irritation surged. "What am I to do? Remain alone and unprotected? The sense of being watched by men who know I am alone is overwhelming. I am scared. Although I can take care of myself, because of kind people like ye and Struan, I remain alone."

"I do not mean to upset ye," Flora said. "By yer lack of

ability to do common tasks, I can tell ye come from wealth and are not used to doing for yerself. At the same time, ye have managed to survive."

Grace blew out a breath. "It is so hard."

"I agree. But ye have work with me and if ye feel unsafe, there is a room above the shop. Ye can move there. We will be closer."

It lessened her fear to know whoever came would have to traverse through the shop and up the stairs to find her.

"I will accept yer offer to move upstairs upon my return. However, I am still compelled to go and speak to the laird. I have to know what happened."

Flora smiled. "I understand."

They continued working, the entire time Grace wondered if she was making a mistake by seeking out a man who never showed up to pick her up. What if he'd changed his mind or had lurid plans for her? After all, she would be at his mercy.

Her thoughts raced back and forth, and she could not figure out what was best to do. Struan had offered to find him. Would that be the best plan? For him to find out what happened and report back to her?

At thinking about him, her cheeks warmed. When she looked up, Flora was studying her.

It was terrible timing because Struan stood at the door.

"Oh that's right, I'd forgotten about yer lessons," Flora said.

"Ye are too busy," Grace said, her cheeks aflame at instantly recalling the kiss just the night before.

"I welcome the break," Flora said opening the door with flourish. "Please come in."

Struan entered, immediately sending shivers down her spine and the most annoying butterflies came to life in her belly. This time instead of fluttering, they seemed to swarm. She placed her hand on her stomach and let out a slow breath.

His eyes swept over her as strong as a caress. Grace felt her skin prickle in reaction. When she met his gaze, a smile played at the corners of his lips.

The man was perfectly aware that he affected her.

"Where do I stand?" he asked, the throaty deep sound resonating deep in Grace's belly. He walked to where Flora pointed, each movement assured and graceful at the same time. How he controlled his well-toned body stole Grace's attention.

Never had someone gotten such a strong reaction from her mind and body. The way she felt around him was strange. Almost as if her body recognized him in a way that made little sense to the mind.

"Grace?" Flora studied her with a bemused expression. "Let us begin."

She stepped on a stool to measure his neck and being almost eye to eye with Struan made it hard to breathe evenly. Several times, Grace had to remind herself to take a breath or else she would pass out.

In contrast, Struan was absolutely still, his expression impassive as he listened to Flora instruct her on how to take measurements. When it came time to measure the span of his chest, Grace placed her hand palm down on it. Then joining her thumb and smallest finger, she counted softly as she crossed it.

Grace was sure her heart would explode at the proximity

between them. His gaze never leaving her the entire time.

"What is the count?" he asked seeming genuinely curious.

"Six," Grace replied, her voice sounding breathless. "I must do yer back, please turn."

He held her gaze for a moment. "Will ye be prepared to leave the day after tomorrow?"

Unsure why he asked, she nodded. "Aye. I will be."

Flora looked to where Grace wrote down the number and then to Struan. "Are ye to stay at the keep for long? I have come to rely on Grace's help. There is so much to do."

WHEN BOTH WOMEN looked to him, Struan only felt Grace's gaze. With her hair pulled back into a hasty bun, the escaped tendrils teasing at the edges of her face, she was a fetching picture. Everything about her was beautiful. The fact the woman was so blissfully unaware of how enticing she was added to her allure.

Glad for the long tunic he wore that disguised his arousal at her proximity, he'd had to picture gutting a hog to keep from groaning out loud.

"I plan to remain but a pair of days. Unless the laird requires me to remain longer."

The women exchanged looks and Flora spoke to Grace. "Are ye certain ye wish to ask that they find him? What if he is not a good man?"

Grace's gaze flew to Struan before replying. "I only met him once. Not knowing makes it difficult to go on daily. What if he turns up? I am promised to him…" She stopped speaking letting out a frustrated breath. "I prefer to know."

Despite agreeing with Grace, Struan wished she'd change

her mind about going. Once the man's name was brought to the laird's attention, it would not be long before he was found.

The fact the man had abandoned Grace was enough of a reason for a good throttling. Struan wasn't sure he could allow him to take the innocent woman unless the man had a good reason for not coming for her.

"Turn," Grace said after climbing back atop the stool. Her clear green eyes meeting his for a moment before glancing down to Flora. "Can ye tell me where to start from?"

The pressing of her hand on his back made his eyes close as he imagined her touch against his bare skin. Her hand spread and joined across from his left to the right.

"One. Two. Three." Her hand continued and she stopped abruptly.

"Goodness, I lost count." She kept her hand on his back, not seeming to notice, then lifted it and pressed it palm down again on his left side.

"When will the tunic be done?" Struan asked her in a low voice, hoping to distract her.

"I am not sure. Three. Four."

"We will meet at the square. Early in the morning."

Her hand hesitated. "I will be there. Do ye think I should bring more than clothes?"

"Aye," he replied, enjoying her hand unmoving, the warmth seeping through the rough fabric of his tunic. "Bring something to eat."

For a moment Grace was silent, he imagined her frowning at attempting to remember what number she'd stopped at.

"Please do not move. I have lost count again."

Flora walked to the adjoining room. "Would anyone like

something to drink?" she asked but left without waiting for a response.

Grace leaned to the side and peered to where Flora had walked out and then resumed her count, this time her hand moving swiftly across his back.

"I am not sure what to do next. We must wait."

When he turned around, she rushed to sit, her hands primly on her lap.

Struan walked to where Flora had laid out two fabrics. "What are these for?"

"For ye to choose," Grace said standing. It was obvious she could not resist. "For yer tunic. Both will keep ye warm when ye ride early or late."

One was a deep brown, the other more of a light grey. Struan didn't care which one was used. The primary use of the item would be for him to cover his body, nothing else.

"Which one would ye pick?" he asked meeting her gaze. "For me."

Her lips parted and cheeks pinkened at his scrutiny. Then pressing her lips together she looked from the fabric to his face. "I think the dark one. Dark colors suit ye."

"I choose that one then."

"Warm cider?" Flora walked in, stopped, and looked at them. "Is something wrong?"

"He prefers the brown," Grace said moving away from him and back to the stool.

Struan nodded. "Aye, it suits me."

Flora smiled. "I see. I agree."

Unfortunately, the next measurements were down the length of his body, something Struan wasn't sure he could withstand without becoming aroused again.

"Start from his shoulder and down to about here," Flora motioned to his upper thigh. "Ye only need to measure the front."

Grace stepped back onto the stool, brows knit in concentration. It was obvious she was not thinking about what she did. Struan supposed her mind was on the upcoming trip to speak to the laird. Especially when her hand lowered to his waist brushing over his hardened staff.

At his intake of breath, her eyes flew wide, her mouth opened, and she jerked backward. If not for him grabbing her, Grace would have toppled to the floor.

"I-I am sor…" Her face turned a bright red. "I was distracted."

"No need to fash yerself, lass." Struan fought not to laugh.

Beside Grace, Flora was not as successful. She let out a bark of laughter. "Are ye going to faint Grace?"

"No. Of course not." Grace pushed his hands away. "It is just that I did nae mean to touch him so intimately."

There was a knock and Flora went to see who it was. A woman hurried with a basket overflowing with vegetables. "This is for ye," she said looking from Flora to Grace. "A warrior asked that I bring these to ye."

"Who?" Flora asked looking through the items. "What did he look like?"

"Bulky. Reddish hair. Said it was for the lass with dark hair."

"Quinn," Flora said with a smile. "How nice."

Grace studied the woman and then looked to Flora. "Why would he send this?"

The woman shrugged. "Did nae say." With that, she dumped the items onto a table and left.

The levity in the room seemed to evaporate. "I cannot accept a gift. I am an attached woman." Grace went to the door as if hoping to call the woman back but didn't seem to see her. "Why would he do it?"

"I am sure Quinn does not expect anything in return," Flora said in an unconvincing tone. "Am I correct Struan?"

When Grace turned to him, he wanted to relieve her of any burden. "I will speak to Quinn and ensure he is aware ye do nae wish for anything further from him."

CHAPTER FIVE

T HE FEEBLE SUNRAYS barely shown in the morning sky and already Grace had been at the village square for a long while for fear of being left behind.

Through the night she'd changed her mind several times about whether to go or not. The last pair of days, Flora had insisted she leave things as they were. "What if him not coming was a good thing? Do ye wish to be with someone forced to be with ye?"

Every time Flora said something doubts rose and multiplied. She'd not slept a wink, tossing and turning, her mind going over every possible outcome.

THE MISTY HAZE that hung over the village gave way and a man leading a horse came into view. Immediately Grace recognized the gait.

Struan continued toward the center of the village, his head turning side to side as he perused the surroundings. Grace ventured to guess the extra precaution, to scan the surroundings were part of who he was. A guardian of the people and a warrior honed for battle.

When he spotted Grace, his head cocked to the side, just enough to tell her he was considering whether or not to approach. In truth, she preferred he did not. As it was, she was torn about what to do, and speaking to him would only confuse her more.

Thankfully, just then a wagon appeared moving slowly. The man pulled the horse to a stop in front of where Struan was. They were the couple who were going to the keep. Grace had met the woman when she came by the shop to introduce herself.

Glad for the momentary distraction, Grace lifted her bundle of clothes and hurried over to the cart.

"Grace, I am glad to travel with ye," Clara Watkins said with a broad smile. "Ye can place yer things there," the woman added looking her over. "Do ye not have a heavier cloak?"

"I will be fine," Grace replied while rounding the wagon to the back. Struan appeared at her elbow.

"Miles," Struan said in greeting to Clara's husband. He then inspected Grace.

"Ye can use this," he said holding up a tartan. "Up ye go." With that, his hands rounded her waist, and he lifted her up to the back of the wagon as if she weighed no more than a feather.

"I cannot take yer covering," Grace protested. "What if ye get cold?"

"I have this." He motioned to the thick fur-lined cloak around his shoulders. "The tartan is for when I have to sleep outdoors or have to wear the clan colors."

Glad for the warmth, she wrapped it tightly around herself and snuggled into the corner of the wagon to keep away from the wind.

"I think I will join ye," Clara declared. "'Tis much too cold up here."

Clara's husband climbed down from the bench grumbling about women and how they constantly changed their minds. When he met Clara at the back of the wagon, his face softened.

At the look between the couple, Grace couldn't help the twinge of envy, she looked to Struan who watched her.

"I will ride alongside," he said to Miles, who nodded.

"Thank ye for the escort."

Once Struan mounted, they began the trek that would take an entire day if the weather cooperated.

STRUAN AND HIS mount were in sync, both seeming to be one as they traveled over the hilly lands toward the keep. Every time Grace stole a glance to him, his attention moved from the foreground to the back.

With the quiver of arrows across his back accompanied by the huge bow, he was every bit as intimidating as any swordsman.

Something must have caught his attention because he urged his horse forward and spoke to Clara's husband. "Take the wagon to the edge of those woods, hurry."

Grace clung to the edge of the wagon while trying to see who came. The jostling brought a gasp from Clara. "Goodness, we will be bruised from all of this." The woman grasped for the opposite side.

Already Struan had put some distance between them and came to a stop atop a rising, his bow at the ready.

Moments later, he relaxed and motioned for them to continue on.

At seeing warriors gather, Clara turned to her husband. "Perhaps we are to have more escorts now."

The men caught up to them, one in particular rode along-side, speaking to Struan. The other three rode ahead of them.

"What happens? Why are ye going to the keep?" Struan asked the young man, who also had a sword in a scabbard across his back.

"The laird wishes for a report of what happens with the western shore."

Struan looked to her and Clara who studied them in return. "I am escorting them to the keep, ye can ride ahead. Our pace will be slower."

The warrior's gaze moved from Clara to Grace. "I am called Lachland and would be happy to ride along and ensure yer safety ladies."

"Ever so gallant," Struan said, giving Lachland a dour look. "Since when?"

"Since ever," Lachland replied. "Do ye not believe it?" It was the first time Grace had seen Struan in a light conversation. It seemed he and the other man were friends. Although Lachland was obviously quite a bit younger.

"How are things on the western shore?" Struan had sent two archers, along with two warriors to follow the trail of a group of men who'd escaped from the cove. From what they'd gathered, while they'd fought the pirates who'd come to the shore, a few men who'd lingered behind had managed to escape.

"We tracked them to near the shore, where the boat is kept. Erik and his men took over. They will patrol the area regularly. They are definitely trying to get to their boat and leave."

"If ye do not wish to go to the keep, I can report for ye,"

Struan said. "Ye have been on patrol for almost a sennight."

Lachland looked to the men ahead. "They have permission to go. Plan to see their families. I wish to see mine as well."

"Understood," Struan replied, studying Lachland. The muscular young man nodded in return.

Although Struan knew Lachland to prefer the company of men for intimacy, it did not deter from the man's strength or character. Struan liked him and could see the young man going far as a warrior.

"Did ye stay at Erik's guard post?" he asked waiting to note any kind of reaction from Lachland.

The warrior's gaze moved forward. "Aye, I did."

The man had history with Caelan, and not a good one. They seemed to hate one another. And yet, it was Caelan who Lachland was with the day Struan had stumbled upon them.

Lost in the act, they did not hear him approach and by the time Struan caught sight of Lachland mounting Caelan, it had been too late to unsee the scene before him.

He'd walked backward behind a tree, looking away and scanning to ensure no one else came upon them.

Not everyone would have taken lightly to the sight of two men together in such a way. Struan didn't care who the men joined with as long as they were good fighters.

Days later, Caelan and Lachland had fought to viciously, several guards had been required to break them apart. When confronted by the leaders, they'd refused to state the reason for the fight.

Soon after, Lachland had volunteered to be posted in Taernsby, while Caelan had remained back at the guard's post closer to Welland. Now, it seemed, Lachland returned to

Welland.

"CAN WE STOP for a rest?" Grace's voice broke his train of thought, her gaze meeting his.

"Aye." He called out to the men ahead instructing that they find a good place to stop. Moments later, they came to a clearing with a stream nearby. Miles helped his wife from the back of the wagon, while Lachland hurried to help Grace.

Struan wondered if the man did not restrict himself to only men, by the way Lachland's hands lingered just a bit longer than necessary on Grace's waist.

Seeming not to notice, Grace thanked Lachland and then the women hurried to find privacy.

"I will keep an eye," Struan said following, not giving Lachland the opportunity to do so.

Moments later the women reappeared, and Struan motioned to the water. "Ye can refresh yerselves. The water is very clear."

"Thank ye," Grace replied lingering just a bit behind as Clara went to join her husband who'd motioned her to him.

"Will the men ride with us the entire way?" she whispered, her gaze moving to where the four gathered after emerging from the woods.

Struan followed her line of sight. "I suspect at some point they will ride ahead." He looked up to the clouds gathering, signaling it would soon begin to rain.

"If it begins to rain heavily, we may have to find shelter for the night."

Her gaze lingered on his. "Where would we stay?"

"There are several places. Duncan and Caelan Ross have a

large home not very far from here. There are rooms saved for warriors, by the stables."

AS STRUAN PREDICTED, the men told him they preferred to ride faster, and he allowed it. They were anxious to see family. They would be able to reach the outskirts of the village near the keep and possibly outride the rain.

Not surprisingly just a pair of hours after they'd set off, the rain began to fall. What at first was just a drizzle soon became much heavier, so Struan led them to a grand stone home.

They went directly to the stables where an older man who knew Struan introduced himself as Creagh and directed a younger man to take care of the horses.

"There are two rooms there,"—he motioned toward a separate small building—"ye can go inside. Ye will find firewood for ye to place in the small stoves. Then ye can remove yer wet clothes and warm up."

The man turned his attention to Struan. "Mister Duncan and the family are gone to the keep."

"I will inform their cook we are here then, and ask that they provide a warm meal," Struan informed his three charges.

He walked with them to the building next to the stables. Clara and her husband hurried to one room and Struan opened the door to the other one. "Ye can stay here."

The room was perfect. It had two beds with a table between them and a small stove for heat.

"Can ye start a fire?" he asked motioning to the stove.

"Aye, I can. Thank ye."

"I will give ye time to change and then come see about ye."

THE FIRE IMMEDIATELY dispelled the chill in the air. Grace peeled off her sodden clothes, as fast as she could and stood shivering in front of the stove. Unfortunately, the bundle of clothing she'd brought was also soaking wet.

Unsure what to do, she pulled a blanket from the bed and wrapped it around herself. Once that was done, she proceeded to hang her chemise over the back of the only chair in hopes of drying it, so she could sleep in it.

Hopefully her dress would then dry overnight once she donned the chemise.

Her stomach growled and she thought of the bread and fruit she'd brought. The bread was probably wet, and she'd already eaten her apple. Obviously, she'd not been fully prepared for travel.

Knocks made her jump, and she opened the door to find Struan, who remained drenched.

He held a basket as he walked into the room. "Our meal."

After placing it on the bed, he studied her. "Why are ye not dressed?"

Grace inhaled sharply at having forgotten her state of undress. Grabbing the edges of the blanket closer, she peered down at the blanket. "All my clothes are soaking wet."

"They will be dry by morning." With that, he peeled off his cloak and hung it on the hook inside the door next to the wet tartan.

His tunic was dry, but his trews clung to his legs. "I will have to remove my boots and trews and allow them to dry."

With that, he bent, untied his boots, and pulled them off. The trews followed and he walked barelegged to the stove where he carefully placed them on the chair's seat.

Her gaze followed his every move, unable to look away from the display of well-toned, muscular legs.

When he removed his stockings and placed them on the floor in front of the stove, Grace tied the blanket in a knot around her chest then grabbed one of her gowns and flattened it next to his clothes on the floor.

Struan added a new log to the stove and the fire burned brighter. "There is only the cook and her helper at the house. Which means they could not allow us to stay in there. I will have to sleep in here."

"In here?" Grace looked to the other bunk. "With me?"

There was a hint of mischief in his gaze when he looked to her. "If ye promise not to take advantage of me while I sleep."

"I would not dare," she teased back. "I promise to remain on my side of the room."

They sat on the floor atop the blanket from Struan's bed to eat. Inside the basket was a large bowl of warm stew, crusty bread, a cup with butter, and a jug with ale.

Alone in a small room, both in a state of undress, while sharing a meal out of the same bowl was about as intimate a situation as one could experience. Grace had wanted to ask if it was possible for her and Clara to share a room, while the men did likewise.

However, neither Clara nor her husband had offered, in fact they'd hurried off before she had the opportunity. Perhaps they figured Struan would sleep elsewhere. She had, in fact, thought he would sleep in the house.

For a few moments, they ate in comfortable silence. Instinctively Grace knew that Struan would not take advantage, she'd felt from the first time seeing him that he was a man who did not mistreat women.

Not that she'd much experience in the world after having grown up in a home with her father, stepmother, and two stepbrothers. Her brothers were much younger and thanks to their mother had little to do with Grace. Her father was a distant man who preferred to spend his time reviewing ledgers or at the tavern with friends than with the family.

It had left Grace to find her own way. She'd spent many days with a local village girl, who'd become her confidant. Although not happy and quite lonely, Grace did not have much to complain about. Her stepmother's constant grumbling was tolerable, except when her father had had enough and decided to marry her off.

Within weeks, Grace was betrothed and ushered to a large boat bound for South Uist. She'd never left her village, much less the mainland of Scotland. And now here she was in a room with a man who was her only protector.

"Are ye ever afraid?" Grace asked Struan, who finished the last of the stew.

He shrugged. "Everyone is afraid at some time in their life. What are ye afraid of?"

Swallowing and blinking to keep emotion at bay, she replied, "Of the future. I could be making a huge mistake."

Struan studied her for a moment. "What do ye expect to happen?"

"That is the problem. I have no idea. What if the man, Gilbert, takes me away? Treats me badly? What if he is angered that I bring his lack of keeping his word to the attention of the laird?"

"Why then are ye going?"

When his gaze dropped to her chest, Grace realized the blanket had slipped. She tugged it up and wrapped it tighter. "I am not sure."

Struan got to his feet and went to the chair. He lifted the chemise and ran his hands over the thin fabric. "'Tis dry. Ye should don it."

For a long moment, Grace wasn't sure why he'd abruptly stood and did not continue the conversation. She stood and took it, then at him turning his back, pulled it up over her head and down her body while allowing the blanket to slip. The chemise did not provide enough cover alone, but it was warm and made a good barrier between her bare skin and the rough texture of the blanket.

"Ye may turn," she said going to the same chair and feeling her stockings. They remained damp.

She moved her dress closer and turned it to the other side and then from her bundle, took out a skirt and blouse, laying the skirt on the floor and the blouse on the chair where her chemise had been.

After touching Struan's trews, she looked to him. "They are still quite wet. The fabric is thick and will require a long time to dry."

"We have all night," Struan replied watching as she placed another log into the fire. "It is quite hot in here."

Grace nodded smiling. "Aye, the stove provides plenty of heat." Holding the blanket over her shoulders, she went to one of the cots and lowered to it. Outside the day was ending, the cloudy day leaving little light to see by.

The rain fell harder, pelting against the room like rocks thrown from the heavens. The wind whistled its eerie tune seeming to circle the small building.

"My goodness, I hope we will be able to continue tomorrow," Grace said looking up at the ceiling.

Struan lay back on the other cot, his hands under his head, not seeming to realize it caused his tunic to ride up displaying a portion of his leg above his knees. "By morning, the storm will have passed us by."

Her throat went dry, and all thought evaporated, her eyes locked on the man's long legs. What would it feel to lay with him and feel his body against hers as she slept?

As much as she tried, Grace could not picture him with a woman, not in the intimate way that men and women are together. It was as if her mind refused the thought that he'd belonged to another.

"Grace?"

Slowly, she returned to reality, her gaze still on his legs. Grace blinked feeling the heat climb up her neck. "Did ye say something?"

"Aye," Struan replied, then adjusted and pulled his tunic down to his knees. "I said that if ye change yer mind about speaking to the laird, ye should not do it."

There were several reasons why Grace would be unable to sleep. The first, of course, was the fact she kept changing her mind about whether or not to speak to the laird and demand Gilbert Duncan be found and forced to keep his word.

Secondly, and more importantly, was the man whom she shared the room with. Everything about him made her overly aware of how easy it would be to throw caution to the wind and follow her raw instincts and give herself to him.

If there was a silent demand from deep within, it was that

she wanted Struan Maclean. Never before had Grace desired something to the point of distraction. It would be madness, to give in. At the same time, would it be worse not to know his touch?

Grace closed her eyes and did her best not to picture Struan completely bereft of clothing. The more she tried, the less he wore in her mind's eye.

"Grace?" How she loved the deep throaty sound of his voice. "Do ye need anything before we go to sleep?"

This was the moment. When she had to decide to be honest with herself and him or forever lose the opportunity of succumbing to desire.

CHAPTER SIX

H E SHOULD HAVE stayed in the house. The cook would not have balked at it. However, he'd not felt right to sleep in comfort while Grace remained in the humbler accommodations.

When he turned to look at Grace on the other cot, her face was a myriad of expressions, going from sadness to longing. It wasn't fair how easy it was to read her thoughts. Although he desired her, he would never cross the line of taking advantage of a woman.

God how he wanted her. Hastily Struan pulled the blanket up to cover himself and the obvious arousal she awakened in him, over and over again.

"What is it?" he asked. "If ye have something to tell me Grace, ye should."

"I find myself overcome by emotions. It is as if I am still adrift at sea. Nothing or no one to hold on to."

Struan had vowed to never marry. He planned to remain without bairns or a wife. Still, he was not heartless and was not so ignorant that he did not recognize Grace stirred something deep within him.

"Come here." He opened his arms. "Lay with me. We can talk."

In a flash, she hurried over, clumsily climbing into bed

with the blanket still wrapped around her slight body. It tore something in him, at her action. It was as if a thick plank around his heart splintered. Struan did his best to push all sentiments aside.

She lay with her back to him, and he wrapped an arm around her waist. The cot was narrow so they could not avoid touching. He thanked God for the barrier of the blankets.

"Now tell me. What is going on in that pretty head of yers?" She shivered and he pulled her closer.

"It is much too personal to share," Grace whispered. "I am not sure what ye will think of me."

"More personal than us laying in the same bed?" he teased. "Ye can tell me anything. I will listen."

Her soft giggle made him smile. "True. This is rather personal is it not?"

The cabin had cooled as the fire in the stove dimmed. He did not wish to move and place another log onto the fire if it meant she'd return to her own bed. Instead, he closed his eyes and memorized the moment. How she felt against him. The way she trusted him without question.

"Grace, ye were going to tell me something?"

"Aye," she said. "Very well. I am going to be honest." She inhaled deeply. "I wish to have ye... What I mean is that I want ye. Ye know? I want... I feel as if it would be something I would later regret."

"Ye would regret being with me and yet ye want me?" Struan was confused as to whether be flattered or feel slighted.

"No," she exclaimed. "I would regret if we did not."

He considered her words, the silence stretching. "My body screams for ye, Grace," he finally admitted. "However, I could never take advantage of ye. Ye are confused and scared. Unsure of what yer future holds."

To his utter dismay, Grace turned to face him. They were but a breath apart, her gaze on his. "I do not expect anything from ye." She wrinkled her nose. "Ye do not wish to be with me?"

"Of course I do." Struan's voice was strained. "More than any woman I have ever met."

At the response, her eyes widened, and her lips curved. "Truly?"

"Aye," he replied, unable to drag his gaze from her mouth. "I am in a constant battle not to act on my desires when around ye."

It came natural then to kiss, their lips pressing tentatively at first, Struan allowing her to set the pace, not wishing to push her and doing his best to keep from yanking the blankets away.

When she deepened the kiss, a moan escaped, and he realized it came from him. Struan took her mouth then, devouring her, tasting her, licking and nipping at her lips, unable to get enough.

Grace's fingers raked through his hair as she gave into the kiss. The blanket slipped leaving only the thinner cloth of his tunic and her chemise as a barrier. He sucked in a breath at her full breasts pressing against his chest, sending trails of fire directly to his core.

Just kissing her felt more intimate than any sexual encounter he'd ever had—few they may have been. With Grace, his hold on resisting her was slipping.

He wanted her. Desired her with every ounce of his being.

With a growl combined of anger and need, he tore the blanket from around her and pushed the one around him away.

It was then, with only his tunic and the thin fabric of her chemise that his thirst for her was somewhat sated.

Grace trembled, overwhelmed with desire, she pushed her body into his.

Struan ran his hands down her back, to her bottom, cupping the round orbs that fit perfectly in his palms. Down to her upper thighs where he pushed up her chemise, to caress the creamy skin.

"Ye are perfection," Struan whispered, then took her mouth again anchoring his hands at the apex of her thighs and roundness, pulling her up and against his sex.

Grace gasped and trailed kisses down the side of his face, then to his surprise, licked the edge of his jawline heightening the already urgent flames of his desire.

"Grace." He groaned her name as if in pain. "Ye must tell me to stop."

Instead of a reply, she looked up at him. "I cannot." Her kiss swollen lips and mussed hair were his doing and he loved it.

"We cannot," he replied. All the while, his palms were moving up and down from Grace's waist to her bottom. "We must not."

Although inexperienced, Grace would make a wonderful lover. In response, her hand trailed down his side and she slipped it under his tunic. The beauty took his mouth again as she caressed him. Up and down she trailed the tips of her fingers from his side down to his hip. Each movement driving him toward madness, until he yanked his tunic off, and then without words, pulled her chemise off.

On the brink of the abyss, he tried once more. "Beautiful Grace, understand that I cannot give ye more than my body." Before they stepped off this cliff, he had to tell her one more time that nothing more could from this.

Seeing the acceptance and desire in her eyes, Struan pushed her legs apart and settled over her. Grace was silent, her gaze on his. When he sucked her left nipple into his mouth while circling the other with the pad of his fingers, she gasped and threw her head back.

First one and then the other pert tip was treated with the same attention of laving, sucking, and nibbling.

Grace bucked up, wanting more so he trailed his fingers up the inside of her thigh. She trembled at his touch. When he slid his fingers through her sex, she shuddered and surprised him by lifting up for more of his touch.

Wishing to see her come undone, he concentrated on the nub between the folds, sliding down to take it into his mouth.

"Ah!" Grace went rigid as a hard release traveled through her. When he continued the sweet assault, she pushed her chemise between her lips and cried out, a second release striking her quickly on the heels of the first.

While she was lost in the abyss of passion, Struan took himself in hand. His rod was so hard it was almost painful. Guiding himself to her opening, he pushed in slowly, then thrust into her moist heat.

Again Grace cried out, this time in pain. Struan could not stop, he pulled out halfway and drove back into her. With each thrust, she relaxed more and more until she began rocking in sync with him.

She was so very tight. And at the same time, she took all of him into her welcoming body. As he moved over her he fought to keep his movements even and not to thrust too hard. She was lost in their lovemaking, her eyes closed, mouth agape, breathing harshly.

They'd gone too far for any regrets, and he began to move faster, in order to find his own release.

Grace's nails dug into his bottom, urging him forward. The knowledge she found the act between them enjoyable sent Struan over the edge.

An inferno gathered at his core, and he was barely able to pull out before spilling into the bedding. As he came, a hard shudder traveled through him with so much force, he almost blacked out.

WHEN LIGHT HIT his face, Struan opened his eyes slowly and upon realizing Grace was no longer in the bed with him, he looked over to her cot. She was fast asleep, curled in a ball, with the blanket pulled up to her neck. Despite the room cooling, she'd moved away from him.

Struan slid from his cot and went to the stove. He didn't cover up, as there was no need. Moments later, warmth and light from the bright fire began to disperse throughout the room. He looked over his shoulder to Grace, who continued to sleep.

A part of him wanted to shake her awake. To demand to know if the night before had occurred or was it a dream? But he was without clothes, there was no denying it. He'd taken her virginity. Had been her first lover.

Raking his fingers through his hair, he let out a breath. He should have resisted. Should have stuck to his self-imposed celibacy.

By the fact that she'd gone to the other bed, she was trying to keep to her word, not to expect anything from him.

Thankfully, his trews were dry. He dressed quickly, then grabbed his cloak and went outside. The fresh air caressed his face bringing back memories of the night before as Struan trekked to the stables, found his horse, and ran his hand down the animal's long nose. "Did ye rest?"

The horse nickered in response. "I did not," Struan told the beast. "I should have slept out here with ye."

"I talk to my horse as well," Creagh called out. "Yer up early."

"The fire went out." Struan walked to where the man stood over a fire in a barrel. "Besides, I do not wish the couple to know I slept in the same room as the lass."

The man looked toward the small building then gave him a knowing look. "Ah. So ye had a hard time sleeping?" Obviously, Creagh thought he'd kept from Grace. He should have.

"Aye," Struan said and looked toward the sky. "Glad to see the clouds have gone."

"Ye will arrive at the keep without problem," the man replied. "Ye should go to the kitchen to break yer fast. I will inform the others to join ye there. They are preparing food."

STRUAN WAS ALMOST finished eating when Grace and the couple walked in. She met his gaze, and her cheeks immediately turned a bright red. If no one suspected something had occurred before, they would now at her expression.

"Can I help?" She turned away to speak to the cook. "Thank ye so much for feeding us."

"It is what Mister Duncan and Mister Caelan would expect," the cheerful woman replied. Then with Grace's help, they heaped food on a pair of platters that were placed on the table.

Grace lowered to her chair, flinching just a bit. Struan swallowed knowing it was due to it being her first time with a man.

A quick scan of the others assured him they'd not noticed, too busy taking food for their plates.

"I have a tea for ye," the cook whispered to Grace, the woman's knowing gaze moving to him. "To help ye travel more comfortably."

Grace nodded, her face aflame.

"I will wait outside. Take yer time," Struan said pushing from the table so that the couple turned from Grace to him. "We leave as soon as ye gather yer things."

He thanked the cook and hurried outside. It was the perfect opportunity to ensure there was nothing of his left in the room, he went to it and found everything in its place. It looked as if no one had been in it. The narrow beds were made and the fire in the stove doused. Over the back of the chair, his tartan was neatly folded.

Obviously, she'd already taken her belongings to the cart, as her bundle was not in the room.

Struan took his tartan and went back out, noting the couple's horse was already hitched to the wagon. Moments later his mount was saddled, and he guided it next to the wagon.

The trio walked out, each holding a small bundle, which

was probably food the cook had insisted they take.

Speaking to the woman, Grace did not see him. He admired the sway of her hips as she walked, her pretty face flushed from the cool wind, her midnight hair pulled back into a long braid.

"She is a beauty," the stableman said coming up from behind him. "One of the loveliest lasses I've seen in a long time."

"Aye, that she is," Struan replied abruptly. "Thank ye for everything."

The man looked from him to Grace. "I can see why ye could not sleep last night." He chuckled and returned to the front of the wagon.

Struan took Grace's upper arm, pulling her a short distance from the couple who discussed where to sit.

"How fare ye?"

The pools of blue that reminded him of the sea looked up to meet his. Then her lips curved. "I feel different. As if walking on air." She gave him a shy smile. "Thank ye."

The last thing he expected was to be thanked. It was not like he'd chopped wood or repaired something for her. "I do not want to be thanked," Struan replied curtly. "I want ye not to regret it."

"I do not. Not at all." Grace patted his shoulder. "I am happy." With that, she turned and walked to the wagon and waited for him to help her up.

Unsure of how to feel about her rather dismissive response to the night before, he walked closer, placed his hands around her waist, and lifted her to the wagon.

She moved to the same place as the day before, taking the tartan he extended and placing it over herself.

The woman, Clara, had decided to sit on the bench next to her husband, leaving Grace alone in the back.

"I am going to regret this," Struan murmured to himself, as he mounted and followed the wagon away from the Ross' home.

IT WAS ONLY a couple hours later that the huge grey walls of the keep came into view. At Carla's prompting, Grace got up on her knees and looked over the side of the wagon to the keep. She turned to Struan, and he rode closer.

"It is so big. I did nae realize how huge Ross keep is."

After so many years of living there, he'd not considered what it would look like to a newcomer. The high grey stone walls and huge home within was always a welcome sight after long treks and time away. Inside, he still maintained a room with his belongings.

Despite being assigned to the guard post at Taernsby, he expected to return to live at the silver castle, Duin Láidir.

"How many people live within the walls?" Grace asked no one in particular. Since he was the only one with the answer, Struan did a mental count.

"The laird, his mother, his wife, and bairns. At times, like now, his brothers Duncan and Caelan are here with their families. There are others who remain permanently.

"About fifty guards live within, as well as servants, horse handlers, gardeners, and village families also come and remain, in tents they pitch on the grounds."

At coming to the gates, they were waved in by guards who recognized Struan. Several of the men peered down with curiosity at the wagon. Obviously, Lachland had already spread the word of a beautiful woman enroute.

Struan growled softly in annoyance. She was a woman of value, not one to be treated without regard.

"To the side there," Struan told Clara's husband, motioning to the side of the huge stables.

Upon nearing the building, lads rushed out to see about the horses.

"Unhitch the wagon. Ensure my steed is brushed down and fed some apples."

"Will ye remain sir?" one of the lads asked before leading his horse away.

"I will, aye. Allow Brutus to roam in the corral. I will take him to his stall later." The lad nodded and hurried away.

When Struan turned, the trio stood next to the wagon. All of them looking around, taking in all the activity.

Following their line of sight, Struan looked across the courtyard. Near the well, several servant women were gathered filling buckets. A short distance away, women sat in the sun, sewing and chatting while a group of bairns ran in circles playing. There were corrals filled with guardsmen's horses, pens with livestock, and several chicken enclosures as well.

To the left of the keep was a grassy area that was used for sword practice. At the moment there were about twenty men sparing, the sounds of metal clashing ringing through the air.

Just beyond where the men sparred, there were tall bales of hay on which targets were pinned for archery practice.

Further to the left was a path that led to steep steps that took one to the loch's edge. To the right of the keep were the gardens. A large vegetable garden next to a flower garden. There were benches and a short wall one could lean on and study the view of the forest and beyond.

He knew that if one stood atop the wall, one could spot the seashore to the east. Salty air circled around them, the freshness of it prompting one to take deep breaths.

"It is like a village here," Grace said bringing Struan to the present. "So much activity. I never expected it."

"Duin Láidir is the largest keep on the Hebrides," Struan said not keeping the pride from his tone. "It is my home."

CHAPTER SEVEN

THE REST OF the day, Grace was kept entertained by all the activity inside the keep. She and Clara walked around the courtyard, wishing to explore every single space until finally, Miles came to fetch them and take them inside.

Upon entering the spacious great room, once again, Grace was awestruck. The ceiling was high and the distance from the entry to the dais was much further than she expected. Rows of long tables with benches filled half the space, while the other half had several circular tables and chairs that faced a huge hearth.

Before the hearth, oblivious to all the noise, two enormous wolfhounds slept. Women sat in the chairs holding conversations, while more sat at the circular tables.

There were blankets on the floor against one wall where bairns were laid to sleep, or play. A few women sat next to them, keeping an eye on the lot.

Tugged by Clara to a table, she turned and looked to the front of the room. At the center, flanked by warriors was whom she presumed was acting as laird.

Just after arriving on the isle, she'd caught sight of Laird Ross, who had a long golden mane, and this man was not he.

The man who sat at the dais, wore tailored clothing, and had light hair a shade too dark to call blond with red streaks.

He had the air of an Englishman.

"Who is he?" Grace asked Clara, who reached for a piece of bread from a trencher on the table.

"Miles says he is Caelan Ross. He often sits in for the laird, despite living on the other shore. Something must have called the laird away."

"Half-brother," a man said from across the table. He lowered his voice. "Bastard born. But never say it in front of a Ross. Ye will lose yer tongue."

Grace nodded, taking heed. The last thing she needed was to get on the laird's bad side.

"Are ye to speak to the laird...er brother?" she asked, out of curiosity.

The man nodded. "Aye, my wife insisted on it. Need guards to come see about our neighbors to the south, who continue to encroach further and further into our fields."

Despite the many people in the room, there seemed to be an order of sorts. People stood in a queue, waiting to speak to the laird's brother, while others meandered at tables, speaking in low tones.

"Why are so many people here?" Grace asked Clara.

Her companion shrugged. "Some await a reply to their request. Others seek shelter for a day or two. Still others travel through and come to pay their respects."

Clara studied her. "Did ye not see yer laird at yer village?"

"No," Grace replied. "When father went to the keep, he took my stepmother and sometimes my stepbrothers. Never me."

If the woman thought her response strange, she didn't say. They just continued sitting, waiting for when Clara's husband reached the front of the queue.

At a serving woman nearing, Grace tapped her elbow. "My clothes are damp. Is there somewhere I can hang them to dry?"

"Aye, go through there,"—the woman pointed to an archway—"to the right and down the corridor are the laundresses. They will help ye."

"Thank ye." Grace looked to Clara. "I will return shortly."

Just as she walked through the archway, Struan appeared. "Where are ye going?"

Despite appreciating his protection, Grace wasn't sure she liked his constant questioning. "To the laundry to see about hanging up my clothes. I do not wish them to mold."

He nodded, "I will show ye the way."

Following his tall figure, she had to admit to feeling safer than wandering about alone. There seemed to be guards everywhere, almost all with expressions of suspicion and distrust.

"Here ye go. After, come and find me. I will get ye something to eat." With that Struan turned and walked away.

He'd not met her gaze, nor seemed at all interested in more than showing her where to go. Grace frowned at his retreating figure. The man went from hot to cold, from friendly to distant from one moment to the next.

A chuckle caught in her throat. Then again, she was no different. Annoyed he questioned her, then when he showed no emotion, it bothered her.

"What do ye want?" A young woman studied her from head to toe. "Are ye to work here?"

"I can help if it is needed," Grace said. "I need to dry my clothes. They are damp."

The girl stared at the bundle Grace clutched. "Ye can wash them there." She pointed to pots with boiling water. "And hang them there." She then motioned to lines that hung from a doorway to outside.

The room was filled with steam and the unmistakable odor of lye. Glad for a way to wash her clothes, Grace hurried to untie her bundle.

"Stir these while I go grab another bundle," the same girl said, and hurried out of the room.

An older woman began to laugh. "Peigi will not return any time soon."

"Oh," Grace said looking to where the young woman disappeared. "I do not mind. I've spent the last two days in the back of a wagon. Need to stand for a bit."

With the help of the other woman, Grace took the clothes from the cauldron, rinsed them with cool water, and then hung them to dry. She enjoyed the chatter of the women in the room as they described how Peigi used every opportunity to chase after one of the guards.

According to them, the guard had begun hiding from her.

She was helping to dump a second load into the cauldron when Struan appeared. The woman instantly went quiet at his appearance.

"What are ye doing?" He frowned at her and the other woman as they held bed linens over the cauldron. "I asked ye to return to the great room to eat."

"Is he yer husband?" one of the women asked, looking to Struan with distrust. "Ye should not allow him to order ye about if he is not."

Struan scowled at the woman. "And it is admissible that

she should be put to work without pay?"

"I do not mind," Grace said, unsure of what to do. She lowered the linens into the cauldron and pushed it down with the paddle. "There." She wiped her hands down the apron they'd loaned her, then removed it and went to hang it on a hook.

"I will return later." With that she walked out of the room, letting Struan follow her.

Struan caught up with her rather quickly. "Ye do not have to work for yer meals here."

"I am aware. Like I said. I did not mind. The women in there are quite nice."

He blew out a breath but said nothing more. Once back inside the great room, the aroma of food and freshly baked bread caused her to almost swoon.

She'd barely eaten that morning, her nerves so fraught her stomach was unstable. The table where Clara sat was full, so she followed Struan to another, where they'd obviously left two spots open for them.

There was only one other woman at the table, and she had the air of being a warrior. The rest there were men. No one paid her any heed as she lowered next to Struan. They continued discussing a recent patrol and the woman joined in.

"Is she a warrior?" Grace whispered to Struan.

"An archer. She is here from Skye, looking to find her brother."

The woman wore her hair in a long braid, her features were sharp, almost manlike, but at the same time, she was beautiful. It was interesting that the men treated her as if she were part of the guard.

"She beat most of the archers, except for Ewan Ross, at archery. She's challenged me." Struan slid a look to the woman. "Layla Maclean, daughter of Laird Maclean."

There was admiration in Struan's gaze when he slid a look to Layla, and Grace wasn't sure she liked it. "Can I attend?"

"Aye, of course."

After the meal, which was the most delicious food she'd ever eaten, Struan went to speak to the laird's brothers. It seemed he had reports to make.

Grace lingered, waiting to speak to Layla, who finally stood and walked in the direction of the archway that led toward the laundry.

"Can I ask," Grace began, getting the woman's attention. "How did ye learn archery?"

Layla's lips curved, softening her features. "By trailing after my brothers and bothering them until they gave in and taught me." She met Grace's gaze. "I practiced every single day until besting them, which of course, they did nae like."

Despite not liking that Struan admired the woman, Grace instantly liked her. "I am glad to see a strong woman take on and beat a man."

Layla nodded. "Come and see me beat yer protector then." With that she continued forward, long strides taking her down a different corridor.

After checking in to ensure her clothes were still hanging, Grace went to Peigi, who'd now returned. "Where can I watch the archers compete?"

The woman's thin lips curved. "Come, I will go with ye."

They exited through a side door to a covered area with a few benches and tables. By the lack of décor and crudely made furniture, it was where the servants went to rest and get fresh air.

However, the view of the archery area was perfect. Grace looked across the field where the family and their guests could sit and thought her view was much better. Unimpaired by banners and such.

Quite a few people sat in the stands. It seemed word had gotten out that the woman archer had challenged Struan.

"Are ye allowed to sit over there?" Grace asked Peigi, who nodded. "Aye, we can. But here is a much better view unless ye are in the laird's box."

Grace agreed. "How many are competing I wonder?"

Her question was answered when four archers walked to stand in a line. Struan, Layla, and two others Grace didn't recognize.

Thankfully Peigi informed her that one was Ewan Ross, brother to the laird and the other was one of the laird's personal archers, named Edward.

The first one to step up to the line was Edward. He shot at a target that had been set up in the middle of a stack of hay bales.

There were exclamations and clapping. He'd hit the center, just a bit to the right. Despite the almost perfect shot, the archer growled in displeasure. The next person to shoot was Ewan Ross. His arrow penetrated the target almost dead center. Layla was next. She stood straight, everyone went silent as she pulled the taut string back and released it.

There were exclamations of excitement and clapping when she split Ewan's arrow. The laird's brother threw his hands over his head in an exaggerated demonstration of being angry, while everyone laughed.

Again those in attendance went silent when Struan walked to the line. His face was stoic and yet his movements were graceful and fluid. He notched the arrow, pulled back, hesitated for a moment, then released it. It was as if the arrow moved slowly through the air as every eye followed its progress.

The arrow landed just to the right of the split arrow, hitting the target exactly in the center.

This time, the audience jumped to their feet.

"It is a rare occurrence that an archer beats a Ross," Peigi said clapping and hopping up and down.

Struan went to where the other three archers stood, and they shook hands. Layla patted his shoulder and said something. In that moment, he looked to where Grace was. For a long moment, he looked to her, but she could not see his expression clearly from where she was.

An announcement was made, and he turned away to face the crowd. Seemed they were to shoot again, this time from a longer distance.

This time, Ewan Ross won, with Layla and Struan's arrows much too close to say who was better. The archer Edward was awarded second place.

Servants came out to the field with tankards of ale, as an axe throwing competition was organized spur of the moment. There was a celebratory feel in the air.

She noted that as the crowd prepared to return their attention to the field, the laird's brother and his guards headed back into the keep.

Grace wondered if Clara and her husband had spoken to

the laird yet. It was best she go see what occurred and ask to return to Taernsby with them.

Walking down a corridor, she became confused as to which direction to head. Hearing voices, she went left and ended up in the kitchens. Women spoke in jovial tones while chopping vegetables and meat.

It was the largest kitchen she'd ever seen, with a large window that housed a myriad of pots overflowing with herbs of every kind.

"It is beautiful in here," Grace exclaimed when getting a woman's attention. "I am glad to have gotten lost."

"Look Greer, it seems the lass is lost," a thin woman said looking at Grace. Several of the kitchen helpers giggled.

"Shush Finella," the woman replied then looked to Grace. "Where do ye wish to go lass?"

"The great room," Grace replied.

The cook got a young lad, who sat in a corner cracking nuts. "Lad show her the way. Then come back straight away."

The boy moved so quickly, Grace almost had to run to keep up. Then with a grin, he pointed through the doorway, rounded her, and sprinted back to the kitchen.

Upon entering the great room, she was once again overwhelmed by the size of it. There were fewer people about and she did not see Clara or her husband. She walked past several tables and looked where the women gathered by the hearth, but Clara was nowhere to be seen.

Finally, she hurried through the front door to the courtyard, crossed it, and went to the stables. The wagon was gone.

A lad was brushing down a horse and Grace went to him. "What happened to the wagon of the people who arrived earlier today? They left it there." Grace pointed to where she last remembered seeing the wagon.

"Many wagons come and go every day, miss. I do nae know."

Grace rushed to find the guard who'd stood by when she'd arrived but couldn't find him. Finally, she returned back out to the field in hopes of finding Struan. Surely, he'd know where they'd gone.

Her heart thundered at not seeing Struan anywhere. Had everyone gone? Surely he'd not leave without at least informing her.

By the time she returned to the great room, Grace was breathless.

"Is something wrong, miss?" She whirled to find herself face-to-face with the laird's brother. His blue gaze taking her in. Her breath caught at the close perusal from a man of his standing. He was handsome, a bit too handsome if she were being honest. She couldn't help but get a closer look at his attire. The fabrics and sewing were impeccable.

"I-I cannot find the people I came with. They came to speak to ye about finding their son." Grace inhaled sharply.

Caelan Ross nodded. "Ah, yes. They've gone. One of the guards seems to know where he may be." With a curt nod, he continued on down a corridor.

Grace ran after him. "I have to return to Taernsby. I came with them."

One of the guards gave her a quizzical look. "For?"

"To speak to the laird," she replied. "But I have changed my mind," Grace quickly added.

The laird's brother motioned to a room. It was a large

study with a table in the center that was intricately carved. In the front of the room was another smaller table with a large leather-covered chair behind it. Along a side wall was a beautiful sideboard with decanters and cups.

Someone pulled out a chair for her and Grace sat. She felt silly in such a nice room, her feet not touching the floor.

"What is it that ye wished to speak to my brother about and changed yer mind?" Caelan asked.

Her stomach clenched. "I was shipwrecked on my way here from my village on the mainland. I arrived later than planned. Someone was to meet me and never came. It was either that, or they thought me drowned and left."

"Why did ye change yer mind?" If only the man would stop asking questions.

Grace struggled to come up with a credible reply. "The man arranged with my father. I was to come and marry him. I no longer wish to marry him."

"If ye are betrothed, by an arrangement by yer father, then ye must."

It was exactly why Grace hated that she'd never been able to tell a lie. If there was ever a time to do so, this had to be it. "I may carry another man's child," she blurted out. Her own eyes widening at the words.

Caelan and the guard exchanged looks, but neither looked at her with judgement.

"I see," Caelan finally said. "Are ye married to this man?"

Her entire body blazed with embarrassment. Why had she said such a thing? "No," she said, her voice barely above a whisper. "I am not."

"Who is he?"

Grace blew out a breath. "I would rather not say."

"Either ye name the man, or I will have to turn ye over to yer betrothed."

CHAPTER EIGHT

S TRUAN'S HEAD SWAM after imbibing so much ale. It had been a long time since he'd allowed himself the liberty of getting drunk. However, it was also a celebration of his accomplishing something rare, beating Ewan Ross.

When he stood to relieve himself, he swayed sideways with each step. Struan chuckled and burped when he stumbled, almost falling.

On the way back to the guard quarters, he was intercepted by Colin MacTavish, one of the head guards. "Caelan Ross wishes to see ye."

"I am drunk," Struan replied as if that explained anything. "Tell him I can barely walk."

"Come," Colin said as if not hearing him. "Now."

Struan shook his head in a futile attempt to dispel his fuzzy eyesight and get his bearings. When walking through the great room, he grabbed a tankard from a passing servant and gulped down the contents.

He managed to arrive at the study doorway, looked to Caelan and then to Grace, who was still as a statue.

Upon Caelan about to say something, he released a booming belch. "Apologies. I am shrunk."

Colin took him by the arm and guided Struan to a chair. "Sank ye," he replied.

"This may not be the best time to speak to ye," Caelan began.

"'Tis the best time," Struan replied placing the tankard on the table with a thump. "What do ye wish to…" He couldn't think of the last word, so he gave up.

Caelan turned to Grace. "Have ye and Miss Durie had relations? Is it possible she is with child?"

"Shile… aye..but nay." Something told Struan, to get up and leave the room, but his legs did not cooperate. "Who?"

"Grace," Caelan said slowly. "Are ye and she…"

"Ah," Struan said turning to Grace whose eyes widened. "She is a lovely lass. My lass. I will not admit it to her." He raised a finger to his lips. "*Shhhh.*"

CAELAN TURNED TO her and Grace bit her bottom lip. Struan was much too inebriated to make sense. Surely the man would not remember anything that occurred once he slept it off.

"I wish to return to Taernsby immediately. Please. Struan… er he, can find me there. He knows where I live."

When a snore sounded, everyone turned to see that Struan had fallen asleep, his head hanging, chin on his chest.

"We will speak tomorrow." Caelan turned to his guard. "Colin, ask Greer to find her a room for the night."

Grace ate last meal with the cook and her staff in a small dining room adjacent to the kitchens. Then she drew water from the well, washed up, and undressed. Climbing onto the cot she finally allowed the fear to take over. Struan would be so angry with her.

What had possessed her to tell such a lie? First thing in the morning, she would go in search of the laird's brother and admit to telling a lie in order to keep from having to marry the man she'd been betrothed to.

Turning to her side, Grace wondered if perhaps it would be a better idea to escape. She could ask for anyone heading back to Taernsby and go with them. Once Struan returned, she'd explain and apologize for lying.

Satisfied that she'd come up with two plans that could work, she relaxed.

THE SOUNDS OF people talking seeped through the cloud of sleep. Grace opened her eyes just enough to notice it wasn't quite light outside yet and fell back asleep. What seemed like moments later, she woke again. This time, the room was much brighter.

"Good. Perfect time to find the laird's brother. Or should I first see if I can find a ride back to Taernsby?" Grace murmured as she got dressed and brushed the tangles from her hair. With efficient fingers, she braided it.

After a quick rap on the door, Peigi peered in. "Ye must have been very tired. I came and took the clothes ye wore yesterday to wash them. Ye did nae even stir."

"I was. But I feel so much better now," Grace said. "Thank ye for it. Hopefully, they will dry before I leave today."

Peigi shrugged. "Not too long before it dries. It is close to the fire."

"I must find out if anyone is going to Taernsby. Can ye help me?"

Apparently, the laundress took advantage of any opportunity to be out and in search of her guard because Peigi nodded eagerly. "We will wait until after the midday meal."

"What about first meal?" Grace asked.

"That was hours ago," Peigi replied, taking her hand. "Come hurry. Ye can break yer fast and meanwhile, I will go out to the courtyard and ask."

"Midday meal?" Grace asked, her eyes wide. "Is it that late?"

"Aye, they are having it now," an oblivious Peigi replied. "The laird finished hearing from everyone that came seeking time with him."

"Oh, no." Grace raced past Peigi toward the great room. Once in the doorway, she peeked inside, hoping to catch a glimpse of Struan. Hopefully, he'd been much too drunk to get up early.

Her hopes were dashed at seeing him at the same guard's table where they'd sat the day before.

His expression was dark, he sat with both elbows on the table looking straight ahead but seeming not to see at all. Grace prayed it was because he had a headache and not that the laird's brother had demanded he marry her.

"Mister Caelan wishes to speak to ye in his study." It was Colin, the guard from the day before who'd neared without her noticing. "Come with me," he said taking her elbow.

There was no way to escape and no other option than to admit the truth. She'd lied and would have to marry Gilbert if he was found.

As they crossed the room and went down the corridor, Grace felt as if she were being led to the gallows. What had she gotten herself into? The one time she'd told a lie and here she was about to stand in front of one of the most important men in Clan Ross and admit to it.

Upon entering the study, once again Grace was taken by the room's feel. It was a comfortable space, and yet the air could change depending on why one was summoned. In her case, her nerves were rattled.

"Please sit," Caelan said. "Have ye eaten midday meal yet?"

Grace shook her head. "I can eat later. Right now I must explain myself."

The men exchanged looks. "Struan explained to me this morning. He's agreed to marry ye."

"No." The word escaped without warning. Grace clapped a hand over her mouth. "I will nae marry a man forced to do it."

"He was nae forced. Came to me this morning and asked that the marriage take place today."

"Why would he do it?" Grace looked to the doorway. "He never wishes to marry. No. I refuse to."

The laird's brother let out a breath. "Ye refused to marry yer betrothed. Admit to intimacy with one of my guards and now ye refused to marry him as well."

Since it was a statement and not a question Grace did not say anything. Instead, she prayed for a way to get out of the predicament. "Can I go and seek food?"

"Not until ye explain what ye plan to do. Why come here in the first place?"

He was right, of course. If not for coming there, she'd not find herself in such a predicament.

"Since the shipwreck, I have not had an easy time of it. I come from a well-established family on the mainland of Scotland. My father sent me away, married me off to this man, Gilbert Duncan, who paid handsomely for me." When her voice faltered, Grace paused.

Colin poured something into a glass and placed it in front of her.

The liquid was smooth, but fiery at the same time. When it settled in her gut, somehow it seemed to fortify her enough to continue.

"I have learned to be more independent. I work and can feed and clothe myself. However, I do wish for a husband and family. It is not easy to be alone when yer a woman, one needs protection. That is why, on impulse, I wished to speak to the laird."

"Then ye changed yer mind?" Caelan asked.

"Aye, I did."

"Because ye care for Struan?"

"Partly, aye. But because I care for him, I will nae ever force him to be with me. He only asks to marry me out of honor. Nothing else."

The room was silent as Caelan considered her words. She looked from him to the guard, who took a sudden interest in his fingernails.

"This man, Gilbert Duncan, I know of him. He will be sent for, and I will speak to him. I will nae tell him ye are here. Then I will speak again with Struan and then I will decide. Until then, both of ye will remain here."

The room seemed to spin. What if he decided that she should be married to Gilbert? Would the man punish her for not being a virgin? Grace squeezed her eyes shut. "Must ye summon him? If he did not come for me, then it is obvious he does nae wish to marry me."

Caelan met her gaze. "Seek something to eat and then find a place to rest. All will be well."

With that, she was dismissed. Grace tried in vain to find something more to say, but the guard moved closer, making it obvious she had to leave.

She'd find someone to take her back to Taernsby. The last thing she wanted was to end up making everyone miserable.

When she hurried past the great room, she looked to the guard's table. Struan was no longer there. Grace wondered if perhaps he'd realized his mistake and had done the smart thing. Mounted and left.

"There ye are," Peigi said at Grace entering the laundry rooms. "I was just thinking about ye and wondering what ye'd be doing."

Grace took the paddle from Peigi and began pushing the clothes down into the bubbling water. "I need yer help," she whispered.

At once there was a mischievous gleam in Peigi's eyes. "Do ye wish to meet a man in secret?"

"Nay. I wish to find someone going to Taernsby or in that direction at least. I must return home."

By Peigi's less enthusiastic expression, she was disappointed in the assignment. However, relieved of having to work, she readily agreed. "I will go ask now."

"Where are ye off to Peigi?" The head laundress called after her, but Peigi was quick and disappeared through the doorway, pretending not to hear.

Quite a while later, after the clothes were rinsed and a new batch dumped into the water, did Grace finally leave to find something to eat. She was very hungry and quite worried as Peigi returned with news that no one was heading toward Taernsby.

The lass did say a guard offered to take Grace in exchange for payment that did not include coin. When Grace gasped, Peigi giggled. "I told him ye would nae do that."

She trudged to the kitchen in hopes of asking for anything left from the midday meal, but upon catching a glimpse of Struan entering from the outside, she ducked into a room and peeked out through the cracked door.

"When do ye return?" the guard with Struan asked.

"There is an issue to be resolved. Not for a pair of days at least. Let Gavin know that Caelan asked that I remain." Struan's voice did not give away anything. Grace gritted her teeth.

"Is something wrong?" the guard asked, and Grace wanted to hug him.

They'd paused just past the doorway where she was, so she could hear clearly.

"Paying for a mistake. A big mistake."

Struan's replay made her heart sink to her stomach and Grace had to grip the doorway to keep from faltering. The men continued forward, speaking in low tones and she no longer cared what was said.

Instead of going to the kitchen, she dashed down the corridor to the room where she'd slept and closed the door behind her. Tears fell down her cheeks at the physical pain in her chest.

What she felt at the moment was the same hollow ache that had consumed her the day she'd embarked on the ship that took her from everything she'd ever known.

The ache that had been her steady companion for the week's long voyage. A shadow that followed her every waking moment. Now it was back, and it was her fault for trusting and allowing herself to hope.

IT WAS EASY to leave the keep without being stopped. So many people came and went, it seemed that the guards barely looked at the people who left. They concentrated instead on those arriving, which made sense.

The man driving the cart gave Grace a quizzical look. "From where I am going it is another two days walk to Taernsby. Are ye sure to wish to go there?"

"Aye, I am," Grace replied looking over her shoulder. "I have to leave."

Just then two men on horseback came into view. One looked familiar. It wasn't until too late that Grace realized why.

"Grace?" Gilbert gave her an incredulous look. "I thought ye were dead."

CHAPTER NINE

S TRUAN WALKED PAST the kitchens and then to the laundry, but he did not see Grace anywhere. Either she was asleep in her room or was hiding from him.

"I may have to demand a rematch," Ewan said when he went out to the courtyard. "The wind definitely affected my aim."

At the man's arched brow, challenging him to argue the point, Struan returned the look. "I beat ye yesterday and I can beat ye again today. It turns out the trickster doesn't always win."

"Ha!" Ewan said. "I demand a rematch then."

"Very well. I must find someone first."

The man walked alongside. "Who do ye seek?"

"A woman. The one who traveled here with me." He stalked past the well, to the stables, then not seeing her, returned to the great room. It could be she returned there.

"A woman?" Ewan said, a bit too loudly. "Ye came here with a woman?"

"Someone seeking to speak to the laird. A couple as well, not just her." It was irritating to feel as if he had to explain. "No matter. Once I look in the great room and find her, I will come to the archery field."

"I will help ye find her," Ewan said, his keen eyes taking

him in. "Who is she?"

"No one," Struan snapped. "Just a village lass."

"I see," Ewan said as they walked into the great room. There were only a few people mingling about. Struan often wondered if some lived there and managed to keep from it being noticed. He doubted it went unnoticed, but the laird let it slide rather than throw them out into the cold.

Colin stalked toward him. "There is something I must tell ye." The guard motioned for him to follow and to his annoyance, Ewan followed as well.

"What is it?" Struan asked, at this point he was about to lose his temper. Not sure why he was angry, other than he wished to speak to Grace, and she was nowhere to be found.

"He returned, yer lass' betrothed, and demanded to know why she refused to marry him. Upon stating he'd made an ironclad agreement with her father, Caelan had no choice but to relinquish her to Gilbert Duncan."

His mouth went dry, and his chest constricted. "When did this happen? Are they here?"

"Nay, he took her away, not even allowing the wee lass to gather her clothing when she asked," the guard replied.

Struan's stomach clenched. "Where is Caelan now?"

"He went to the village," Colin said. "Left me here to find ye and inform ye that ye do not have to marry the lass after all."

"Marry?" Ewan asked with a look of surprise, eyebrows high. "That is news."

"What was Grace's reaction?" Struan asked, turning toward the stables, both men in tow.

"Upset. Said she did nae wish to marry Duncan. Caelan is

bound by the agreement her father made and for the payment received. There is nothing to be done now."

When Colin placed a hand on his shoulder, Struan stopped. "Ye can nae go after her. She cannot be yers."

Struan let out a long breath. Unsure of what to do, he looked toward the archery field. "I feel as if I have failed her."

THE COMPETITION AGAINST Ewan was not a challenge in the least. Struan only managed to hit the center of the target once, and it was on the very edge of the red circle. Ewan, who would have normally gloated, barely said a word.

After, Struan went to his room in the guard quarters. He was free to return to Taernsby but was not motivated to do so.

His room in the guardhouse was small, with barely enough space for a bed, a table, and a chair.

There was a rap on the door and a young archer, Ian, peered in. "Do ye wish to go to the village with me?"

Not wanting to be alone with his thoughts, he agreed. A short time later, they mounted and headed to the village as the sun fell below the horizon.

They arrived at his parents' home, and Ian smiled broadly. "Mum is making a huge pot of stew and asked that I bring a guest. I believe she was hoping for a lass, but ye will do."

Struan shook his head. "As long as she does nae think I am yer lass."

"There is very little chance of it," Ian replied with a grin as they led the horses to a small but tidy stable.

The house was warm and Ian's family welcoming. Struan had always enjoyed visiting with Ian, but it had been a long time since he'd done so.

Ian's mother hugged and kissed his cheeks, and her husband waved him to come sit and tell him all about what happened at Taernsby. The man loved to hear warriors tell of their *adventures*, as he called them.

Soon they surrounded the table, along with Ian's younger sister and brother. The family was jovial, one talking over the other, telling Ian of all the things he'd missed while being gone to Taernsby. Both parents offering to speak to the laird and ask that he be given work at the keep.

Struan watched the interactions in silence, admiring the relationship Ian had with his family. It was so foreign to him that such a thing existed, genuine love between parents and siblings.

Even the laird's own family had suffered greatly under the late laird's hand. Thankfully, the lack of paternal care had brought the seven siblings closer. Now they'd all settled into loving marriages and would, in Struan's opinion, have families such as this.

"What of ye?" Ian's mother asked. "Do ye plan to remain in Taernsby for long?"

He'd not considered it. Not since realizing he'd not see Grace again. "I am not sure," he replied honestly.

"Ye and Ian both belong here. Close to the keep where I can ensure ye eat properly." The woman chuckled reaching to cup his jaw. "Ye look sad, lad."

At the comment, Ian looked over and shrugged as if to impart his lack of ability to control his mother.

"I am well. I assure ye," Struan replied.

It was decided—for them—that they would remain there for the night and after drinking Ian's father's whiskey, there was no arguing.

THE FOLLOWING MORNING, Struan woke to the smell of meat cooking. He sat up from his place on the floor where he'd slept on rather comfortable layers of blankets.

"Ye are the first one to rise," Ian's mother said with a smile. "Once ye are ready. There is hot porridge and pork bits. Ian likes to have this when he is here."

To Ian's credit, it was a delicious combination. The sweet porridge offset the saltiness of the cured pork. Struan ate with gusto, then kissed the delighted woman, who made him promise to return soon.

As they rode away, Struan turned to Ian. "Ye are fortunate to have such a good family. I am glad ye invited me."

"Aye, I hoped it would lift yer spirits. I hate being away but have to admit to enjoying the returns more now than when I came more often."

"It is good that ye do not take it for granted." Struan guided his horse out of the village and toward the keep.

Ian scoffed. "Never. When I decide to marry, the woman will come visit my home often to see what kind of life I expect. Not to say it is perfect, because it is not, but I wish to have a caring family of my own."

"I hope ye do. But do not tell the lass, ye expect it. Women would not like to be compared. Each person has to be their own."

"Ye have a point. The lass will have to understand from what she sees," Ian said, making Struan shake his head in amusement.

When the keep came into view, immediately all the

warmth of the visit evaporated as he considered what to do about Grace.

What happened to her at the moment? Was she being mistreated? What would happen when her betrothed discovered she was no longer a virgin?

Despite the fact he never wished to marry, neither would he allow harm to come to Grace. She did not deserve to pay for his lack of control over his body.

The lass was an innocent and he was wrong to have taken her despite what she said.

Struan stalked from the stables after leaving the horse to the lads and went in search of Caelan.

To his surprise, Darach had returned. The Lion, as he was called, stood in the middle of the great room surrounded by clans' people vying for his attention.

Caelan sat at the dais, so Struan rounded the crowd and went there instead.

"A word," Struan said without preamble. "In private."

"If it is about the lass, there is naught that can be done. She has gone with her betrothed."

"Why did he not show up to fetch her upon her arrival?"

"He stated that he was told the ship had wrecked, so he assumed she was dead."

Struan considered what to say next. "Ye believed him?"

At this Caelan met his gaze. "The lass agreed that the man and she were betrothed. She was put aboard a ship to come to him. What the circumstances were upon her arrival, had nothing to do with the original reason for her being here."

What the man said was true. However, he had to know more.

"What of the fact she is no longer a virgin? Was that discussed?"

"Of course not," Caelan snapped. "I understand how ye feel, however, ye yerself said ye do not wish to marry but would because ye had to. Now ye do not have to."

It was useless to argue the fact. Struan knew it, but he couldn't help but wonder about what would happen to Grace.

"Where does Duncan live"

"North, near Gideon's lands. Do not go there. It is an order. Ye will return to Taernsby in the morrow with Ian and the rest."

Unless he wished to be punished, Struan had no choice but to obey. "Aye," he said between clenched teeth and walked out of the room to his own.

LATER THAT EVENING, Struan grabbed clean clothes and went to find a place to bathe.

There was a bathing room attached to the stables and it being late, no one was there. Struan lifted the kettle from over the ever-present fire and poured it into a large wooden tub, then he added cold water. He stood naked in the tub and poured water over himself, washing with soap that was made in the village while considering what to do.

While shivering as he dressed, Struan came to the obvious conclusion.

He had to give up and let Grace go. She was never his, nor meant to be his.

The sooner he went on with his life, the better. This was to be the same lesson he'd learned early in life. Never allow feelings free reign, nothing good came from it.

Ever.

TWO DAYS LATER, Struan rode through the village square at Taernsby and stopped at the seamstress shop. He dismounted and tethered Brutus, who pawed the ground, seeming to be in as bad a mood as his rider.

When Flora opened the door, she looked past him. "Where is Grace?"

"Her betrothed came to the keep and took her."

"Oh, no," Flora replied distraught. "Poor lass. She must be so scared."

"Why would ye say that? She came here to marry him. I would think it was precisely the outcome she'd wish for."

"Ugh," Flora gave him a droll look. "Do ye really not see it?" She walked to the table where Grace usually sat and shook her head sadly. "Grace did nae want to be with him, not after meeting ye. She is quite attracted to ye and was nae sure what to do about it. I think the main reason she went to the keep was to spend time with ye."

Struan wanted to deny it, but he'd suspected the same. After what had occurred between them, it had been especially hard not to go after her.

"There is naught to be done. He paid a bride price for her."

"So pay him and get her back." Flora gave him a little shove. "Please leave, I am very angry with ye," she snorted. "I can nae believe ye allowed her to be taken."

Mounting again, he rode from the village north to where he'd be on patrol for the day. Despite there being little activity at the cove, they continued to keep an eye just in case some of the people returned.

"Struan, over here," Lachland called and waved him over.

A couple stood next to the warrior looking quite scared. They had to be young, perhaps ten and six at the most.

"What are ye doing here?" Struan asked looking to the rather sad-looking shelter they'd built.

"We wish to be together, ye have no right to stop us," the lass said, her face set. "Go away and let us be."

The lad gently pushed her behind him in a protective way. "We are in love and wish to marry. Headed to find the vicar in Taernsby."

It would take them half the day to walk to the village. They were right in stating there was little warriors could do to stop them. "Lachland, escort them to Taernsby. They can ride Brutus."

He dismounted and walked to the trees where other warriors had started a fire to keep warm.

As he stood with the other men, he couldn't help but wonder what Grace was going through at the moment. The way of marriage was so unfair to women. Decisions about who they'd spend their life with was decided by men. Most times, they'd end up married to someone they'd met but once.

He looked toward the direction of where Lachland had gone with the couple. The families had probably not agreed with the union, so they'd been forced to flee and marry. The young people were brave. They'd probably either remain in Taernsby or return to their homes to announce being married.

"Oy!" an archer called down from a platform atop a tree. "A ship arrives."

Immediately, several others including Struan climbed up rope ladders to catch a glimpse of the arriving ship. Through the branches, he spotted the vessel. It flew no flag, which wasn't a good sign. When it turned and headed to the cove, he called out to the rest of the archers to get in position.

A scout was sent to the guard post and the remaining warriors disappeared into the trees.

The fire below continued to burn, with only one guard sitting near it. If whoever came ashore made it that far, they'd not think much about a single man keeping warm.

The ship continued forward slowly, heading directly at the entrance of the cove. Struan itched to reach for his bow, but first they had to determine if the people aboard were friend or foe.

Whoever manned the ship knew about the cove and wanted to avoid the more populated areas, however, that only told them they did not wish to be seen.

It could be they were smugglers or pirates. Either way, whoever they were they would have to answer many questions.

A short while later, the ship stilled. At the same time, Gavin rode into view and waved to Struan motioning for him to come down.

"They are here," Struan said. "What do ye wish for the archers to do?"

"We will wait for the first ones to come ashore. Take them and find out what business they have coming to our shore."

With a plan in place, he joined the line of warriors hidden on both sides of the narrow pass through the trees.

He and Gavin stood at the cove's entrance watching the small dingy, with six men, come ashore.

The men jumped from the dingy, pulling it ashore. Then they stood looking toward the boat, while one waved both arms.

A man on the ship waved back and they turned to walk into the trees. The six then pulled out short swords and walked away from the shore.

"Wait," Gavin whispered and motioned for the others not to move. They waited until the men were out of sight of whoever remained aboard the ship before stepping out from the trees and surrounding them.

Caught off guard, the men froze. One who gave the impression of being the leader growled in frustration and lifted his sword.

"There are archers in the trees that will ensure yer sword never lowers except when ye are dead," Gavin said.

The man looked up to the trees where archers with notched arrows were perched.

"Ye understand what I say then?" Gavin asked. "What are ye doing here?"

The man glanced over his shoulder to the others. "We come to trade with the people here. Mean no harm."

"Then why dock in a hidden cove?" Struan asked meeting the man's narrowed gaze. "If ye wish to trade, then it would be best to go to a more populated area."

Without speaking, the men from the ship dropped their weapons and held their hands up in surrender.

"Ye will be escorted back to yer ship. This is yer only warning. Return and we will not hesitate to kill." Struan said, pushing one forward to walk.

When the party emerged onto the shore, those on the ship watched silently as the men hurried to the dinghy. The six rowed back to the ship where they were helped aboard.

Moments later, the ship left and disappeared.

"Go to the keep," Gavin told one of the warriors. "Inform our laird of what occurs."

"Can ye see them?" Struan called up to the men who remained on the platforms. An archer affirmed they could and called back that the ship headed north along the shore.

"Why do they head north? We must keep an eye on them." Gavin motioned several men forward. "Ride along the shore. Ensure to keep track of the ship."

"I will go with them," Struan said. "We do not have time to get more men."

THE SHIP WAS fast, but the warriors managed to keep it in sight. As the sun fell and gave way to darkness, they'd reached the keep where a second set of warriors took over, following the shoreline. The ship was not far from the shore, it was visible by the lit torches aboard.

Struan was exhausted and fell into a fit filled sleep without so as much as a bite of food.

WHEN MORNING CAME, he went to the kitchen to break his fast.

"The laird is needing to speak to ye," Greer, the cook, informed him. "What have ye done? I heard it has to do with ye courting a lass. A man is here about it."

Struan looked to the ceiling. Had the couple from Taernsby come to insist he marry the lass Lily? "I have nae been in a place long enough as of late to court anyone."

"That is what I said," Greer replied with a snicker. "He must be mistaken. It is well known ye are never in the company of women. Except for the lass, Grace. Quite bonnie she is."

"When did the man come?" Struan asked, hoping to steer the conversation in a different direction. "What does he claim I owe him?"

"Earlier today. Is probably still here somewhere. Not sure what he expects from ye. He is wearing well-tailored clothing."

At the description, it was obviously not Lily's Da.

After eating, Struan went to the great room where only a few people were about. It seemed the laird and family had not risen yet.

Colin entered the room, his brows rising at seeing Struan. "Ye are here."

"Aye, following the ship." Struan looked around the room for the man who Greer described as older with well-tailored clothes.

"A man claims to be offended. Not sure what he expected as he did nae bring the lass back here with him. Of course, we did not tell him it was ye."

Struan whirled to face Colin. "I am not understanding. Who is the man that is looking for me?"

"Gilbert Duncan. He came to speak to the laird, wishing for whoever defiled his betrothed to be punished."

Struan's blood ran cold. "Do ye know where he lives?"

"The laird wants to talk to ye."

Struan turned on his heel and ran out toward the stables.

Moments later, he mounted and went in search of Grace. If the man had harmed one hair on her head, he would not hesitate to kill him.

CHAPTER TEN

T HE DREARY WEATHER outside matched the interior of the home. Grace supposed the house could be described as lovely, if it wasn't for the starkness within the walls. Even with the fire in the hearth, the rooms remained cold and drafty.

"Make yerself useful," a gravelly voice repeated—yet again. "Ye should do more than just stare out the window."

The old woman tapped her cane against a table leg for emphasis. "Do something. Bring me some hot porridge." She was Gilbert's mother, who by all appearances, was not well-liked by the servant hired to care for her as she was nowhere to be found at the moment.

Grace slid a look at the scowling woman and walked out of the room to find the kitchen. The entire time praying she would not run into Lilith, another woman who also lived there.

"Where are ye going?" Unfortunately, Lilith appeared from a doorway and peered down her pointy nose at Grace. "Skulking about looking for something to steal?"

For whatever reason, Lilith and Gilbert's mother had taken an immediate dislike to Grace. She guessed it was because they hoped he would marry Lilith and her sudden appearance meant he may not.

"I cannot think of anything I'd want to steal from this

place," Grace replied continuing on her trek.

Lilith caught up with her. "Ye should leave."

Gritting her teeth, Grace turned to her. "I agree. If ye would kindly arrange for a carriage, I will be on my way."

"Impertinent." The woman huffed, turned on her heel, and walked away.

It was a horrible situation. Not only was she not welcome there, but upon arriving, had been questioned by Gilbert in the most embarrassing of ways.

He'd demanded to know why she'd been hiding from him, then abruptly changed his tone and insisted he'd searched for days in hopes of finding her alive. When Grace informed him she preferred to leave, once again he'd become angry.

"And go where? Will yer father return the money I paid? What of the monthly trips I made to the keep?"

"I will repay ye," Grace had offered, eliciting a cruel laugh. According to the maids, the man only went to the keep for the food and gossip, not as an effort to find her.

"With what?"

Thankfully, the conversation had been interrupted by Lilith, who always found a way to interfere when she and Gilbert were together. Which fortunately suited Grace just fine.

MOMENTS LATER, GRACE sat near the fire while the old woman drank her porridge and then promptly fell asleep.

There was no way to escape. The house was situated quite a distance from the nearest village. Grace had kept track of the direction they'd traveled, certain they'd gone north and far from Taernsby.

"Where did he go?" Grace asked a maid who entered to clear the plates and add a log to the fire.

"To the keep, I believe," the woman replied with a soft smile. "He was quite angry."

Grace frowned. "Was he?"

The man had demanded she come to his bed and Grace had refused. When he'd asked why, she'd repeated the lie: That it was possible she was with child.

At that, Gilbert had flown into a rage and called her a whore. To his further annoyance, Grace had been unaffected by it. She'd expected it. After only a few hours in his presence, she concluded, the man had never moved past being a coddled boy.

Gilbert Duncan was older, perhaps forty, with graying temples and silver throughout his hair. He was short in stature, which he tried to distract from by hitching his chin upward.

He had a medium build, with dark close-set eyes and thin lips. As if to add insult to injury, a prominent mole took residence on the right side of his nose. She's not sure how she missed that the one and only other time she had seen him.

Grace went to the window again, pulling her shawl tight around her shoulders, and peered out. There were fields that were dormant at the moment, a forest to the left, and a road that led from the house to a second crop of trees.

It was impossible to see past it. To the right was the stable and another outbuilding, which she assumed was a pen for livestock.

Lifting to her toes, she noted there were a pair of horses. From what she could see whoever looked over the livestock was not about.

It was her opportunity to escape. Gilbert had left the day before and was probably still at the keep, or just leaving. If she rode straight south, perhaps it would be possible to get to Taernsby and hide from him.

Grace doubted he'd come after her. After all, what did he care, other than the lost money, Gilbert seemed to prefer his mother and Lilith's company to hers.

In the short period she'd been there, Grace had learned the man was manipulated by his mother. In hopes the old woman would agree for Grace to leave, she'd gone to her and asked. The woman's dry cackle sent chills up her spine.

"Gilbert will nae let ye go. He paid good coin for ye and so ye belong to him."

"I refuse to marry him," Grace had said to the woman, who chuckled.

"That is good because I do not wish for him to marry ye. A lover aye, but not a wife. Ye are not the woman for him."

"I will nae lay with him. I belong to another," Grace had spat out the words, satisfied when the woman's mouth fell open.

"What do ye mean?" Lifting a bell, she'd rung it loudly until a maid appeared. "Not ye!" the woman screamed. "Gilbert, come at once."

And so they'd questioned her again and this time, it was decided by his mother that Gilbert should go see the laird to demand whoever defiled Grace be severely punished.

She'd refused to name Struan, telling them it had been a farmer's son. Someone she'd met outside of Taernsby. The more she weaved into the tale, the angrier the duo became.

The old woman had tried to hit Grace with her cane but missed. "Ye are unworthy."

GRACE LOOKED UP from the window.

The old woman stared at her. "My son deserves so much more than ye… better than ye."

Grace replied with a huff. "Ye hold yer son in much too high a regard. Where I do not. Not at all."

"Get out of my sight," the old woman screamed. "Get out."

Glad to have a reason to walk away, Grace hurried to the back entrance. She took a cape from one of the hooks and walked out into the cloudy day.

Within moments, she mounted one of the horses and rode away, unsure of where she was headed, but knowing it was better to be lost than to remain in Gilbert Duncan's home for even one day longer.

WITH NO SADDLE or reins, it was hard to guide the horse and after a short distance, Grace began to lose hope. The confused horse weaved its way down a path through the trees, then turned and headed back to the house.

Grace pulled at the animal's mane until it finally turned away from the house. She kicked both legs and the horse eventually picked up its pace. Frustrated at the lack of distance, she hoped the horse would keep the faster pace.

The animal had other ideas. After a few minutes, the horse slowed and then began nibbling at grass.

"Ye are the worse horse ever," Grace said, feeling silly sitting on a horse who was enjoying its meal and did not pay her any heed.

Sounds of men's voices made her heart thud and she scanned through tree branches. A pair of riders came into view, they rode straight past. Neither was Gilbert.

As soon as they were out of earshot, Grace tugged at the horse's main and kicked its sides. Thankfully, the horse decided to cooperate.

WHEN SHE ALMOST fell off the horse from sheer exhaustion, Grace could only guess, but she thought she was still far from Taernsby. For the last few hours, all she'd seen were trees and one village.

From Taernsby, it had taken more than a day to get to the keep. From the keep to Gilbert's house, almost another day. If she were to guess, it was possible that she was close to the keep.

Instead of continuing to Taernsby and possibly getting caught by Gilbert, it could be that she could go to the keep and ask for asylum.

No. The laird's brother had already come to a decision. He'd decided she had to go with Gilbert as he'd paid the bride price. Had things changed when Gilbert returned to demand to know who'd been with her?

Grace looked up to the starlit sky praying for an answer about what to do.

The crunching of leaves made the horse turn, its ears twitching.

"I agree, let us continue," Grace whispered.

When arriving at the edge of the woods, the salty air made Grace realize she'd been heading in the right direction. In the distance, a rider came into view.

At once she recognized Brutus, Struan's blond horse. Unsure of what to do, her decision was taken away when her mount noticed the other horse and took off at a trot toward it.

"No. Stop!" Grace yanked at the horse's mane in vain. It only served to annoy the horse and it picked up the pace.

Struan noticed her at once. He called out something and turned his horse in her direction.

Upon nearing, he took her in. "What are ye doing?"

"I am leaving that man's house and returning to Taernsby." Grace met Struan's eyes, hoping her thundering heart did not give away how happy she was to see him.

His green gaze moved from her face down her legs and then back up. "What happened to yer cheek?"

Reflectively she reached up to touch the tender spot. "A low branch. This horse is most uncooperative and has led me through rather narrow paths."

"I see." His lips twitched just a bit. "Ye stole a horse?"

"Borrowed," Grace replied. "I am sure it will know the way back home."

Struan dismounted, walked to her, and held up his hands. "Get down from there."

It wasn't the most graceful of dismounts. Thankfully when she went sideways, Struan caught her.

Upon ensuring she was steady on her feet, he went to his horse, retrieved a rope, and made a makeshift bridle for her horse. "Ye will ride with me."

"Where exactly are ye planning to take me?" Grace asked. Although she could not outrun him or keep him from taking the horse, she could fight against being taken back to Gilbert.

Struan frowned. "It is best ye go to the keep."

Her heart sank at knowing he would willingly turn her over to someone else rather than try to convince her to go with him. Why did she suddenly feel so hurt? They'd not made any promises to one another. And Struan had repeatedly said he would never marry. None of this had changed.

When a tear slipped down her cheek, Grace quickly wiped it away. "What I really wish is to return to Taernsby. To my little room and to work with Flora. I do nae wish to be sent somewhere by the laird. He will be duty bound to return me to Gilbert."

"Did the man mistreat ye?" The muscle on the side of Struan's jaw flexed. "Did he?"

Grace shook her head. In truth, the man was angry, which he had every right to be, but he'd not mistreated her. "Nay. But I do nae think he will marry me now. He knows I have been with another. I believe he intends to keep me as his lover and marry another."

Struan looked past her toward the sea and then in the direction in which she'd come. "I can take ye to Taernsby, but he will find ye there."

"I would rather take my chances than return to his home and be kept as a lover by a man I do not care for."

Both she and Struan were well aware, she really had no choice in the matter. Her father had sent her to Gilbert. Whether he married her or not did not affect the fact she belonged to him now. If Struan took her away and was caught, he could be punished.

THE SOUNDS OF birds settling into trees above and the dimming light as the end of the day approached meant they had to decide soon in which direction they were to go.

Wordlessly, Struan lifted her to the saddle and mounted behind her. He then guided the horses toward the keep. Grace wanted to argue, to fight against the fact he was to turn her over to the laird, but she was thirsty, hungry, and exhausted. Instead, she hung her head and waited for the inevitable.

Once inside the keep, they crossed the courtyard and kept going. Moments later, Struan dismounted and helped her down. He then spoke to lads, who came and took the horses away.

"Come, quickly," he pulled her by the hand toward a building, opened the door, and pushed her inside.

It was hard to tell what the space was until he lit a lantern. The small room was simple but with all the basic necessities.

"This is my room. Ye can rest here. I will go and fetch ye something to eat." He looked at her for a long moment and then pulled her against his chest. Grace let out a shuddering breath.

"I do nae know what to do about ye, Grace," Struan said.

"Help me, please," Grace replied.

He left a moment later without making any promises. It did give her hope that he was considering how to help her since he hid her away from those in the main house. Grace went to the tidy cot and sat down.

The Ross guards had nice accommodations. Each man had his own, albeit small, but private space. There were a few things on a small table, a leather-bound book, a wooden bowl that held small items, and a carved wooden horse.

At hearing men's voices outside, Grace held her breath. How long would she be able to hide? The first place Gilbert would look for her would be the village.

There had to be a way to keep from him.

An idea struck, but she pushed it away. Then she stood and went to stand by the table. Lifting a thin leather strap, she ran it across her palm while thinking.

It could work, all she had to do was convince Struan. If he agreed, she would be out of Gilbert's reach and safe from having to ever be taken from the life she chose.

The only downside was that she'd have to give up all her dreams of ever having a family of her own.

CHAPTER ELEVEN

WHAT THE HELL was he doing? Struan walked into the great room and searched again for the man, Gilbert. At a table he noticed someone who had to be him. The man sat alone. Other than a pair of men, who were on the opposite end of the table.

He walked over and sat down, not looking to the man. When a maid walked by, he motioned her over and asked for ale.

"Are ye here to speak to the laird?" he asked Gilbert, whose narrowed gaze met his.

"Do I know ye?" the man replied.

Struan kept a blank expression. "I do not believe so. I am head archer to the laird."

"I already spoke to the laird. Had hoped for more information, but it seems there are more important things as my request has been ignored."

The servant returned with ale and a tray with bread and meat. "Greer wishes to see ye."

Maids had eyes and ears everywhere, he was sure word that he'd brought a woman with him had already reached the cook. He nodded to the maid.

"Perhaps ye can help," Gilbert said. "I am betrothed to a woman who is not…how can I put this…worthwhile."

"And what do ye expect the laird to do?" Struan asked, fighting every instinct not to punch the man in the face.

"I wish to know who the man is. She refuses to tell me. The laird could find out and punish—"

Struan interrupted. "Ye should return her to her family. Be rid of her if ye no longer hold her in high regard."

"She was given to me as payment. Her father owed a great deal of money to several men who threatened his life. I told him that I would take care of it in exchange for the lass. She is comely."

The fact Grace was used as a commodity made Struan's blood boil. It happened quite often that women were used as payment. Some were horribly mistreated, but a lucky few managed a rather normal life.

"I see. So ye paid off the man's debts?"

"It was a matter of saying a few things that made them give up on collecting the debt. In actuality, she was quite a bargain." The man chuckled. "The only thing that made her worth anything was her virginity. Now that is gone." He shrugged.

"There is naught to be done about it now."

"Aye, there is." Gilbert's face contorted with anger. "Something was taken from me. Stolen. I will be repaid. I will return home and do what I have to and find out who it was."

With that, the man drank down the contents of his cup and belched loudly.

Struan pushed away from the table. "Ye are right. The laird has much more important things to see to than yer quest for who took a woman's virginity." He got up and walked away.

"Struan," Darach said coming from the direction of the

kitchen with a tart in one hand. "Are ye to remain here or return to Taernsby?" The laird seemed in good spirits.

"Can I speak to ye privately?" Struan asked.

"Aye," the man continued on through the great room. Struan followed him to his study.

Once there, the Laird waited for him to speak.

"I am sure ye have been told about the man out there, Gilbert Duncan, and his request that whoever defiled his betrothed be punished."

Darach took a bit of the tart and chewed while nodding. "Aye," he said in between chews. "I am told it is ye."

Struan stalked to the sideboard and motioned to the whiskey decanter. "May I?"

At the laird's nod, he poured two glasses and gave one to the laird. He then downed the contents.

"I offered to marry the lass. Then she was taken by him. Now he is asking for me to be punished because he wanted a virgin. The man does nae plan to marry her." The conversation was awkward as he'd never had to speak of his private life to anyone. For his entire life, he'd done well in staying away from women and from dealing with any issues that came with courting and such.

Now he was caught in a situation from which there was little to be done. The only way to help Grace, if he decided to do so, would mean a permanent attachment.

"I accept that what happened should not have. I will marry the lass before I allow someone to take her as a lover. No doubt mistreat her because of my lack of self-control."

When the laird laughed, Struan wanted to hit him. "Ye act as if marriage is no different than being led to the gallows and hung. I assure ye my friend that it is not."

Struan took a fortifying breath. "I never wished to marry. I do not want a family or any bairns. I do not think my mind will ever change in that manner. If I marry Grace, she will have to agree to it."

The laird took the glass, drained it, and held it out for a refill. He ate the other half of the tart whilst Struan poured the amber liquid into the two glasses. Then he met his gaze.

"How is it better for her that ye marry her then? I can nae allow it, not when ye only do it to keep her from what ye have decided is a worse fate."

"She asked that I take her away."

The laird looked up to the ceiling. "Ye have her?"

Struan wanted to slap himself for the slip. "Aye. Some-where safe." He proceeded to tell the laird about the trip to the keep and admitted that she'd come to ask for Gilbert to be found.

But that she'd changed her mind. "Upon him showing up, for his monthly visit, Caelan made the decision to give her to him."

"Sit down," Darach stood. "Not only did ye sleep with a woman that ye were escorting and who was on her way to ask that her betrothed be found, but ye've now absconded with her?"

When Struan went to speak, the laird held up his hand to stop him. "And now ye are gallantly offering to marry her, in name only, in order to keep her from her betrothed."

"I cannot offer more," Struan said. "Ye must understand. I am not able."

"Ye choose not to, which is very different." The laird motioned to the door. "I will speak to the lass in the morning. Do not dare take her away."

Dismissed, Struan stalked from the room and to the kitchen where Greer had already prepared a basket with food for Grace. The woman must have seen the expression on his face because she barely said a word.

UPON ENTERING HIS room, Grace stood from where she sat on his cot. She was lovely in the dim light, her expression hopeful.

"Eat and then ye can rest. I will sleep on the floor over here," he motioned next to the small stove.

Grace sat at the table and ate, seeming too hungry to talk until almost done. "Is he still here?"

"Aye, he is," Struan replied. "He is quite angry."

"I will nae go with him," Grace said, her troubled gaze lifting to him.

Unsure what to say, he blurted. "I will fetch water from the well for ye to clean up before bed. Greer included a clean chemise in the basket, under the towel there."

While she looked on, Struan grabbed the bucket and left. The cool air hitting his face was a stark reminder that if he'd not come across Grace, she would have arrived alone and possibly been given over to Gilbert by now.

He looked toward the large house. If he married Grace, would it be possible to keep from her? What if she came to be with child? Whether or not he wanted it, he would end up tied to her for life.

The thought of it made something in him soften but he pushed it away and he ran both hands down his face.

"WHEN I WAS a little girl, I loved sleeping next to the fireplace on the floor," Grace told him as they lay in the dark room. "Not only was it the warmest place in the house, but also, my little dog, Asha, would always join me."

He enjoyed listening to her voice. "I had a dog too when I was young."

"And yer parents? Did they allow ye to sleep with it?"

"I lived alone most of my life. Taken in by one family or another until I was old enough to make it on my own."

"I am so very sorry. What happened to yer parents?" Grace climbed from the cot and came to kneel beside him. To his dismay, she touched his shoulder. "Did they die?"

Struan swallowed attempting to put into words his story. "My father killed my mother after finding her with another man. I am told she was found dead in the house with me in there. I was perhaps three. My father went after the man. They fought and the man killed him."

"Ye lost both parents in one day." Grace lowered to sit on the floor. "Did ye not have any other family?"

He'd never shared the story and it was strange how easily the words flowed now. As if something inside him wished to get it all out. "My mother had one sister, I lived with her for several years. When she died in childbirth and her husband remarried, I was sent to live with another family."

He could make out the outline of Grace's face, her soft expression making him warm. "Come here, ye must be cold." He held out his arms and she quickly lay next to him settling into his embrace.

"The family that I went to live with when I was about seven or eight years of age, only wanted me for what I could do. I was forced to work in the field. Some days I was fed, other times not. I slept in the stables with the animals and had only rags for clothes. When I was ten, I ran away."

"What happened then?" Grace asked, the warmth of her breath fanning his neck and sending trickles of awareness through him.

"Then I did what I could to do for myself, survived however I could. When ye are invisible ye are witness to the worst."

"Oh, Struan. Ye deserve to be happy after all of that."

He chuckled without humor. "How do ye think I can find happiness?" The question was something he wanted to hear her answer to.

"Having a place to call home. A real home. With a…"

"A wife and bairns?" He couldn't keep the bitterness from his voice.

"No," Grace said. "I was going to say with a faithful dog and plenty of good food."

A dog. Struan was truly surprised at her suggestion. She'd not inserted her needs into what she thought would make him happy. He considered it. "A cottage with a dog would be nice."

"There ye go. Feel free to do so. When ye are happy, I will be glad for ye."

"What about ye?" Struan asked, pressing his lips to her hair. "What would make ye happy?"

"Mine is harder to achieve," she finally said.

"Can I help ye?" Struan asked.

Grace let out a long breath. "I do not think so. I thought so, but now I know that it is up to me alone to see about my future."

She pressed a kiss to his neck, her hand sliding down his

chest, an obvious invitation that he would rather die than deny.

Struan turned to her, taking Grace's mouth with his, needing her more than he needed the air he breathed. She was perfect in every way and if there were any way within him to be hers, he would not hesitate.

"Be with me. Do not think," Grace whispered between kisses. "Be with me."

He pulled her closer and ran both hands up her legs, lifting the shift she wore. When she raised her arms, Struan removed the item, leaving her naked. He then quickly removed his own clothes as well.

Never in his life had he felt such silken skin. He pulled her against him loving the feel of every inch of her against him.

She pressed her lips to his and Struan took them greedily, suckling the pink morsels. Grace wrapped her arms around his neck pulling into a tighter embrace. With each happy moan she made, arousal surged within. Struan would have to take her soon. It was either sink himself deep into her, or release atop her.

Sliding his hands down her velvety skin, for a moment Struan could only marvel in the sensations of her body against his, her skin under his palm and her breath fanning across his face. There was nowhere better on earth he could conceive being in that moment.

"Grace," he whispered, trailing his lips down the side of her neck as he cupped a plump breast. When he circled the tip with his tongue, Grace gasped.

While fondling one breast, he took the other's tip into his mouth, allowing his tongue to do all the work for him. He moved across to the other breast, stopping only when she pulled his face up to meet her gaze.

Face flushed, breath in pants, she gazed into his eyes. "Take me now, I fear to be unable to keep from losing all control."

Struan could not deny her. "I wish ye to do exactly that. Allow yerself to come undone."

Lifting her leg over his hip, Struan entered her inch by inch. Her tightness enveloped him, wrapped around his staff drawing him deep.

Grace let out a long moan of satisfaction at their joining and she pulled his face down taking his mouth. The way she kissed him, with so much desperation, was almost his undoing. How the woman had managed to penetrate his defenses was something he couldn't figure out.

In that moment all he wanted was to be inside of her, to move with Grace in sync with what their bodies demanded.

As he drove into her, every ounce of his being demanded he claim her as his. Struan rolled her onto her back and pulled her arms over her head. "Wrap yer legs around me."

When her legs entrapped him, he gave up control, pumping in and out of her, faster and deeper.

The world spun and still Struan couldn't stop moving. The way she arched up, the display of her long throat offered to him. The way her breasts bounced in tempo with his plunges. All were like a magical potion that he greedily drank from.

Darkness threatened at the edges of his consciousness and still he continued thrusting, not slowing even when Grace shuddered, lost in her own climax.

It was as if he raced to catch something just out of his

reach. Suddenly, his body seemed to burst into flames, and he barely managed to pull out before shattering into hundreds of pieces.

"Struan," Grace's voice penetrated through the fog of the hardest climax he'd ever experienced. He struggled to lift his head. "Ye are heavy."

With her help, he slid to lay beside her and pulled her close. As much as he desired her, there was one thing he was sure about. It would be impossible to remain with her without losing his heart in the process. What if he allow it, allowed her in? He squeezed his eyes shut. If he allowed her in and she betrayed him, he would be shattered for the rest of his life.

WHEN GRACE AWAKENED. She was alone in Struan's room. He'd placed her on the cot and had gone out, after pressing a kiss to her temple.

She sat up and looked around the room. It was warm as he'd kept the fire in the stove burning all night.

Today she'd have to speak to the laird. She'd made up her mind to ask Struan to marry her in name only. But after learning his story, she could never ask it of him.

Every part of her rebelled against the idea of leaving Struan, of never seeing him again. However, there was no doubt in her mind, that if she returned to Taernsby it would be torturous to see him and not be part of his life. Which of these outcomes could her heart withstand? Which would be the most unendurable?

The only thing she was sure of right now was that she hoped the laird would take pity on her and allow her freedom.

After dressing, she walked to the courtyard and then to the

kitchen entrance. Once there, she ducked inside and found Greer and her team hard at work. Porridge was being ladled into bowls, while yeasted bread was pulled from the oven and plopped into baskets.

A young girl carefully placed spoonfuls of butter into small bowls as she chatted with another who placed them onto a tray.

"Greer," Grace called out as a woman weaved around the table passing her with a curious glance.

"Aye, lass, come here, ye will be trampled."

"I am not sure where to go," Grace said. "Should I go to the great room?"

The bright-faced woman shook her head. "Struan asked that I keep ye here until he fetches ye."

With that, the woman gave her a gentle shove to the tall table where food was being prepared. "Help with the porridge."

CHAPTER TWELVE

FLORA PEERED OUT the window toward the village square. Another day since Grace was gone and once again she wondered what happened to the poor girl.

As much as Flora prided herself on her independence, there were days, like today, that she was lonely. Thoughts of her life prior to the shipwreck would flood her mind. Her husband's smiles when they chatted as she did the mending; his smiles when she scolded him for barging inside in muddy boots, again; his smiles while he watched her breastfeed. He'd been so proud of his son.

Now they were both gone, she hated to think about it. About what had gone through his mind as he drown. How he'd clung to their son and tried to swim, but a wave had pulled him further out to sea.

Losing sight of them Flora had swam in the icy waters until she'd been pulled aboard a small boat. The men had rowed in circles, finding others, the entire time Flora screaming out her husband's name.

The tightness in her chest made her turn away and grab her cloak. Then she walked the familiar path to the village graveyard and stopped at finding the spot where her husband and son had been buried together.

"I was looking for ye," Gavin walked to where she stood,

and Flora had never been so happy to see someone. "I am going to the tavern to eat, would ye like to come with me?"

She smiled at her friend. "I would like that very much." Flora placed her hand in the crook of his arm. "What are ye doing in the village? I thought ye were busy patrolling the cove."

"We have been. And I will be there all day tomorrow." Flora had become accustomed to Gavin's presence. Although younger than her by perhaps five years, he was a serious man with an even temper. Gavin had been the one to fish her out of the water. He'd held her while she grieved the loss of her family and helped her set up her shop and begin anew.

If there was a man she could love as much as her husband, it was Gavin. She was aware that he saw her only as a friend, for which she would always be grateful.

"Gavin," Flora started. His dark gaze slid to her. "When do ye plan to settle down? Marry. Have bairns?"

His lips inched up at the corners. "I am waiting for the perfect woman."

Flora couldn't help but feel a bit relieved. "There is no such thing. Ye will be alone forever."

"Ah, ye do not know my ability to seek out the impossible," Gavin teased. "Sit. I will order for us."

The tavern was quite busy, and they were lucky to find two empty places near the window. It was the coolest area, which was why it remained empty. Away from the hearth in which a huge fire roared.

Travelers had hung their cloaks to dry on hooks near the fire, giving the tavern a shadowy look.

Nevertheless, laughter and conversation filled the space,

and it was just what Flora needed. She watched as Gavin weaved through the room to the front where he spoke to the woman behind a tall wooden bar. He stood out from those around, a head taller, dark waves resting on his broad shoulders.

When he turned, both men and women followed his progress. He was the leader of the guard and respected in the village.

After placing a cup of hot apple cider in front of her, he lowered to the seat opposite. "They will bring roast pig and bread in a moment."

"Thank ye. I was hoping for company today. I miss Grace," Flora said as she noted a young woman who watched with interest from another table. Her eyes pinned to Gavin.

Gavin frowned. "I have nae heard from Struan as yet. I expect he will return any day now. Perhaps Grace will return with him."

"Grace has gone to be with her betrothed. Perhaps she's married now. I pray she is well."

He had no reply and Flora was glad that Gavin was not the type to say things just to make her feel better.

When the food was brought, they ate in companionable silence, with Flora doing her best to ignore the woman who continued to watch Gavin's every move.

"Have ye noticed the redheaded woman?" Flora asked in a low voice.

Gavin met her gaze. "I have. Hard not to."

"Do ye know her?"

This time his gaze slid to look at the woman, whose eyes narrowed. "I do."

When he didn't elaborate, Flora didn't have to ask. Obviously, something had occurred between the two and now the woman was not happy to see him with her.

"Perhaps ye should speak to her. It is rather uncomfortable the way she watches ye."

Gavin let out a long sigh. "I have spoken to her. She wants to marry me."

The air left Flora's lungs and she looked to the woman, who finally realized they talked about her because she looked a bit surprised, her eyes widening. She recovered quickly and glared at Flora.

"Goodness." Flora looked down at her food, tore a bit of bread, and chewed it. "And I assume ye do not wish to."

Gavin gave her a droll look. "If I did, then I would not be sitting here with another woman whilst she glares at me from another table."

Without meaning to Flora laughed. "I am sorry, but it is quite strange. To be the object of jealousy."

"Ye should nae be surprised. Ye are a beautiful woman Flora," Gavin said, his expression serious.

It was the first time Gavin had complimented her and her breath caught. Flora swallowed and lifted the cup to her lips to avoid having to meet his gaze.

They finished their meal, thankfully the redhead and her companions had already walked out.

"What are ye to do now?" Gavin asked as they walked back toward her shop. Flora didn't thread her arm through his, suddenly feeling a bit self-conscious.

"I have some hems to sew until I get sleepy. Now that my belly is full I may not last very long."

She looked up at him. "Are ye riding back to the guard post?"

"Aye, like I said. I have patrol tomorrow. I only came to the village to visit with ye."

The statement was a matter of fact. The way he always spoke without any undertones that would make her feel uncomfortable.

"I am glad for it. Ye have good timing. I was feeling a wee bit low." They arrived at her door, and she lifted to kiss his cheek just as he turned. Their lips met and to her consternation, Gavin did not pull back, but instead cupped her face and deepened the kiss.

Then he straightened pressed his finger to the tip of her nose and smiled. "Sleep well Flora." With that, he turned on his heel and walked away.

Flora stood in the doorway unable to move. What had just happened?

"Just friends," she murmured while unlocking the door. "A friendly kiss." Except to her, it was more than that. It was what she'd daydreamed about since meeting him. Gavin was not only kind and patient but her constant companion and good friend.

A warrior rode past, and she called out to him, "Ian, any news about Grace?"

The man slowed his horse. "I believe she was sent away with her betrothed." The man waved and continued riding toward the tavern.

Her heart sank. Why was love so impossible? Grace was in love with Struan and could do nothing about it. She was in love with Gavin, but he was younger than her. Would he find her lacking in a few years?

With a long sigh, she walked inside and closed the door.

CHAPTER THIRTEEN

"**W**E CAN SPEAK later," Struan said to Colin, who'd asked what he planned to do. "I must find Gilbert Duncan."

Colin blocked his path. "Have ye considered what exactly ye will do? He has no idea who the lass was with. If ye expose yerself, he will have every right to demand restitution."

"Should I hide then?" Struan looked past Colin's shoulder to where Gilbert sat at the same table as the day before. "I will nae hide."

"What of the lass?" Colin said, once again moving to block his path. "What will happen to her if he decides to publicly shame her in front of the clan?"

At the statement, Struan faltered. Since he didn't know Gilbert, it was hard to tell if he was the kind of man who took pleasure in others' humiliation. From what he gathered, just by him coming to the laird with such a stupid complaint, the man was an idiot.

"Fine," Struan said turning away and walking to a nearby table. "What do ye suggest I do?"

"One of two things," Colin replied. "Ye forget about the lass, or ye fight for her. If ye decide to fight, then ye must marry her."

Why did marriage have to be the answer to everything?

Struan nodded. "I will consider it."

Colin's expression turned to one of confusion. "I hear she is with ye, here at the keep. Ye do not have much time to consider."

"I will speak to the laird." Struan slid a look to where Darach was speaking to a group of people who'd come requesting an audience. It seemed the conversation was concluding, by the way everyone began stepping away.

Without thought, he got to his feet and approached the laird, who gave him a curious look. "Where is the lass?"

"I must speak to ye. It is important."

Despite there being quite a few more people expecting to speak to him, Laird Ross always preferred his men. "Very well. What is it?"

"It is about Grace. The lass who…"

"Do ye wish to turn her over to him?" Darach interrupted.

"No." Struan let out a breath. "I wish to marry her. All blame is mine and I am accepting responsibility. I will pay restitution to him if he requires it. Though without knowing who I was, he admitted not to have actually paid anything for her."

Laird Ross was silent. "I will speak to both ye and the lass in my study. Bring her there after I speak to him." He motioned to the sitting Gilbert. "I am sure we can reach a solution that will suit all of ye."

"Can I be present when ye speak to him?"

"No."

First Struan went to the kitchens as he was sure to find Grace there. When he entered, she sat in the adjoining room, shelling peas.

Her gaze moved to him, a soft smile brightening her face.

"Grace, please remain here. I have spoken to the laird, and he wishes to speak to ye. First, he will be speaking with Gilbert."

She paled. "He is still here?"

"Aye." Struan tried to gauge her reaction to that fact and what she planned to do.

"I will speak to the laird and tell him I will nae go back with him voluntarily. I will escape. Run…away…" Grace looked around as if already planning her way out.

Struan closed the distance, cupped her face, and tipped it up. "I have told him ye and I will marry."

"Why would ye do such a thing? Ye have nae desire to be tied down. Much less to me." Grace looked about to cry. "I could never do that to ye."

He bent at the waist and met her gaze. "If there was anyone I'd ever wish to marry. It would be ye."

"No," the stubborn woman insisted. "In time ye will resent it and hate me. I will nae marry ye."

When she crossed her arms, it was all he could do not to pick her up, throw her over his shoulder, and carry the prideful woman to the chapel in the keep.

"Ye have two choices," Struan told her. "Marry me or marry him. Those are yer choices."

She looked about to cry.

At Colin's appearance in the doorway, he reached for her arm. "Come, the laird wishes to speak to us."

STRUAN GUIDED HER out through the kitchen door, so they did not have to go through the great room.

Why hadn't she listened to Flora and stayed in Taernsby? None of this would have happened. All because she'd let her infatuation for Struan lead her to make such a rash and stupid decision. Now they faced what could possibly be his worst nightmare.

They walked down a short corridor and into a bright room with windows along one wall that gave a view of an inlet below.

Despite the situation, Grace couldn't stop herself from rushing to the windows to look out at the breathtaking view.

At her movement, a black dog rose from its spot by a hearth and wagged its tail.

"It's the laird's dog, Albie."

"Oh." Grace wasn't sure what to do. Her father's hounds had never been particularly friendly. They were kept outside with the other animals.

This dog was huge with rich black fur. It approached her and lowered its large head as if in greeting.

At once Grace was enchanted and placed her hand on his head. "Ye are so well behaved."

"Albie is a good hound," a rich voice replied.

The laird entered the room, next to him was a beautiful brunette, who she recognized as Lady Isobel, his wife. Shocked that the couple came to speak to her, someone with no social standing, Grace instinctively moved closer to Struan.

"Please sit," the laird said and motioned to a grouping of plush chairs.

As soon as they sat, a servant walked in. She poured honeyed mead for her, and the laird's wife and the men opted for whiskey.

It seemed strange to her that Struan didn't seem to think it odd that the laird took time to entertain him as if he were almost an equal.

"Darach trained with most of the guards while growing up. They are not just the clan's warriors, but childhood friends as well," Lady Isobel explained. "I hear ye find yerself in a bit of a quandary."

"Aye," Grace replied, surprised at how comfortable she felt in the woman's presence. "I have made a mess of things."

The laird and Struan remained quiet, listening to her speak. Again, Grace wasn't sure what to make of it.

"Yer betrothed wishes to have ye back. Why do ye not wish to go with him?" the laird asked.

A blazing heat rose from her chest up to her face and she looked to Struan and then to the laird. "I-I am not... I cannot be with him."

"Do not make her say it," Isobel scolded her husband. "It is obvious they are in love." She turned to Grace. "If ye have been intimate with Struan, then ye should marry him."

Grace pressed her lips together. She wanted to marry Struan, but not when he never wanted to marry. "He will resent me for it."

Lady Isobel got to her feet and stood over Struan. "Why are all men so headstrong about marriage? Ye are no different than the others. If ye do not marry Grace, she will have no choice but to go back with a man who may not marry her. She will live a life of disgrace."

"I already agreed to marry her," Struan replied in a low tone. "It is she who refuses."

When he slid a look to Grace, she felt bad to have put him

in the situation they were in. "Tell her," he urged.

Lady Isobel turned to her, and Grace nodded. "It is only because I do not wish to force him. Why can I not seek asylum somewhere, perhaps a convent..."

At this, the laird's bark of laughter broke the tension in the air. "I can nae see such a headstrong woman as a nun."

The laird motioned to his wife to sit. "Struan and I will go see Gilbert Duncan and explain that I've decided that Struan and ye will marry. Struan has agreed to it. The marriage will take place tonight."

When the men walked out Grace downed the honeyed mead. When the laird's wife offered hers, she drank it as well. "I should have stayed home."

They stood and looked out at the view as Grace told the woman all about how she'd ended up there. When she'd told her about running away and the awkward ride on the wayward horse, they'd ended up laughing about it.

It occurred to Grace that if not for the difference in their stations, she would have loved being Isobel's friend.

"Ye will be happy with Struan," Lady Isobel said. "Darach often worried about him and his lack of interest in a family. Of all the men he grew up with, Struan is the one who never had people who cared for him. It is not that he is against having a family." The woman stopped and thought before speaking again.

"I believe he is afraid. Struan has never been part of a family and will have to learn to be a husband and later a father with ye."

Grace nodded. "I know of his past. He has told me. I truly do care deeply for him, which is why I have fears of my own. I do not wish to disappoint him when things are not as good as he deserves."

"Come, let us find ye something to wear. I think ye will be surprised at how Struan will change once he's married. From the way his gaze follows yer every move, I think he will never allow ye to be taken away from him."

"YE ARE TRULY fortunate," Peigi exclaimed circling Grace. "Not only with such a bonnie man, but with this gown."

It was true. Grace could not think of a more beautiful dress than the soft green creation the laird's wife had gifted her. She'd insisted it was one of many she and her sister had brought with them from their home, and no longer wore.

She ran her hand down the soft fabric, recalling the many times she'd asked for a new dress and her father had denied her. In the end, she'd taken some of her mother's dresses. But they grew faded and worn after years of use. It was only once a year that she'd been allowed to visit the seamstress for a pair of new dresses and other necessities. Each time, under her stepmother's supervision.

Interesting that it was now that she had less money that she'd acquired much nicer clothing. First a pair of dresses from Flora and now this one.

"Are ye ready?" Peigi asked. "They asked we come down to the chapel."

"Yes," Grace looked at her reflection in the mirror. With her hair brushed away from her face and pulled up into an intricate arrangement, she looked so very different. She leaned closer to the mirror. The woman who stared back had an uncanny resemblance to the one portrait she'd seen of her mother.

They hurried out of the room and down a corridor to the right. Grace had not been to that side of the keep. Once they exited, there was a serene garden, which they passed and continued on until coming to a small chapel.

A young lad stood by the door, opened it, and spoke to someone. Upon her entering, the few people inside stood.

Grace hesitated at the scene. In front, next to the vicar, was Struan. He wore a blue and green tartan—the clan colors—pulled over his shoulder and pinned in place. Under it, he wore a dark brown tunic. She recognized the fabric.

His gaze met hers with reassurance, giving her the fortitude to continue forward. With each step, it was as if her heart thundered harder and harder. At her breath catching, she had to remind herself to take another.

Soon she reached the front of the room and stood next to Struan. With her head reaching only to his shoulder, she could not slide a look to him to get a read on his expression. However, his presence alone was all the reassurance she required.

As the vicar droned on about the reason for marriage, she lifted her face to look at him.

Struan slid a look to her and hitched his left brow as if scolding her for not paying attention. That he could find a light instant during the moment that would change the course of their lives, was good. She let out a relieved breath.

It wasn't until they were pronounced husband and wife, and Struan placing a chaste kiss to her lips, that Grace took notice of who all was there.

The Laird and Lady Ross, Caelan and Ewan Ross, as well as

many of the guards, were in attendance. Her gaze moved past them to a lone man sitting toward the back. Gilbert Duncan had remained to ensure they did indeed marry.

His flat gaze met hers for only a moment before Grace looked away.

Peigi and several of the other laundresses were also there, as well as Greer and two of her helpers. The women smiled cheerfully when she turned to them.

Struan took her hand and placed it on the crook of his arm. Together then, they walked out, and Laird Ross and his wife congratulated them then walked away.

"We have something small for ye," Greer informed them. "In the kitchen."

A WONDERFUL MEAL of roasted pig, root vegetables, and steamed pudding was enjoyed by the group of servants and the guards.

Between the cheerful conversations and delightful meal, it was strange to Grace how this day had turned out.

Barely remembering her mother, and her stepmother barely acknowledging her existence, Grace hadn't any dreams of a wedding day. Unlike most of her friends, who shared their hopes for handsome husbands and beautiful wedding parties, Grace had not expected much.

Her lips curved when Struan and two guards threw their heads back in laughter at something they shared. Although the people celebrating with them were mostly strangers to her, it was more than she'd ever dreamed.

"Ye are tired wife," Struan told her with a wink. "I think it is time for us to go to our room for the night."

"Room? Ye mean yer room at the guard quarters?" Grace fought off a yawn.

"Nay. We will stay here in the keep tonight," Struan replied.

To her consternation, once again her cheeks heated. "Oh."

Everyone clapped and made cheerful sounds as he took her hand and led her from the room.

CHAPTER FOURTEEN

"TELL ME HOW ye feel," Grace asked Struan as she untied the laces of her dress. Underneath she wore a chemise, which she planned to sleep in. "How are we to go forward?"

Struan pushed her hands away. "Do ye wish to have a conversation or would ye rather I do something more enjoyable with my mouth?"

"I-I do not expect ye to fulfill any kind of act out of duty." Grace stopped talking when the dress slipped from her shoulders, past her hips, and then slid to the floor.

"I do expect ye to stop thinking and allow us to enjoy this night," Struan said, taking her mouth with his.

Her mind went blank. She knew there were so many questions. So many things she needed to tell him. But she couldn't remember a thing.

The kiss, the way his mouth demanded more from hers made Grace clutch his shoulders to keep from falling backward. How was it possible for this man to affect her so?

Struan's body emanated heat, and she reveled in the feel of the muscular arms around her. There wasn't a place safer than when she was with him. It was as if he built a world where they could be alone, and no one could ever harm her.

When he pushed away to yank his tunic off, Grace opened her eyes and watched as every inch of his beautiful body was revealed to her.

First the flat stomach, the ripples up from there to his wide chest and thick muscular arms. His lips curved just a bit when he noticed how she watched unabashedly.

After removing his boots, Struan stood upright and unlaced the front of his trews, then pushed them down at the hips. There were two distinct channels that formed a V from the sides of his hips to the apex at the top of his sex.

A light shading of dark hair covered the skin from where his erect staff jutted out. Two strong muscular thighs were visible next that tapered to well-formed calves.

She would never tire of seeing him bare. He was so perfectly formed, even with the visible scars. One, a slash across his left shoulder. The second, what looked to be a healed cut just above his right hip.

"Ye are perfect," Grace said waiting for him to close the distance between them. When he did, she let out a sigh and lifted her face to him.

Struan didn't kiss her. Instead, he lifted her chemise up and over her head. The heated gaze traveled over her exposed skin, and it was as if he touched her. Her body came to life, her breathing hitched and when his eyes lingered between her legs, she was instantly aflame.

With quick movements, Struan lifted her up and placed her atop the bed. "I must have ye."

"Yes," Grace replied, unable to think of anything more than to be joined to her husband. To become his wife in every sense of the word.

His. Only *his*.

Struan took his time. First, he trailed his tongue along her neck before making his way down to her breasts where he circled the tip of each lightly while his hands glided across her stomach and thighs. The fluttering touches sending streams of heated joy down to her toes.

As much as she was eager for him, Grace wanted this part to last forever. The part when they couldn't think further than what would happen in the next moment of pleasure.

"Oh!" Grace exclaimed when his hand moved to between her thighs, pushing them apart. Every single nerve aware of what he did. In the next moment, when he suckled at her right nipple, she lost all thought.

The collision of his hot mouth at her breast and his hand traveling up her thigh turned everything upside down. She raked her fingers through his hair while dragging her other hand down his back. He let out a deep moan, the sound bringing another source of delight to her already overwhelmed senses.

Then he drove a finger into her, his mouth moving to the other breast. Grace's legs went lax, her body demanding more.

To her shock, Struan began making love to her with his hand. The finger was joined by a second one that he thrust in and out, mimicking what he'd done with his staff. Grace gasped, unable to wrap her mind around what happened, especially when he took her mouth with his, and rubbed himself against her side.

It was the most wonderful experience of her life.

"This is so good." His heated words blew into her ear.

Just as she was about to reply with an affirmative, Struan's thumb moved over the nub between the folds of her sex, and she gasped at the sensation.

"Oh!" she called out when once again he touched the sensitive part.

Struan thrust his fingers into her, rubbed himself against her side, sucked in her pert nipple, stroked his thumb, and she lost all control. A bright light seemed to burst into many more behind her closed eyes and her sex pulsed in a glorious release.

Climbing over her, Struan took her then. He pushed into her slowly just as she floated back from where she'd flown. His stretching, throbbing, and rubbing her insides when he finally impaled himself fully was so deep inside she felt herself fall once more. And this time she went to new heights that she didn't return from for a long while.

MORNING CAME AND Grace woke to find that Struan remained asleep. She studied him for a long while, wondering what the days ahead would bring. He'd refused to have a conversation the night before, insisting it was to be a day of celebration and enjoyment.

She had enjoyed both the meal that had been so thoughtfully prepared and what followed once they were alone was beyond description.

It must have been quite late by the time they'd fallen asleep. They'd made love, talked about the day and the meal, then had made love again. The second time, it was slower and somehow just as sensual.

Grace leaned closer and snuggled against Struan's warm body. Her mind awhirl with questions. What had Gilbert demanded in return for releasing her from the betrothal? Why had he attended the wedding?

The biggest question that loomed, was how Struan felt

about being married. Despite what Lady Ross had said, Grace had doubts.

She closed her eyes, enjoying the feel of their closeness, the sounds of Struan's breathing filling the room. Outside, birds sang in greeting to a new day and Grace inhaled deeply thankful despite all the uncertainty that filled her.

Moments later Struan stirred and yawned. He turned to her with an unreadable expression. "Ye have been awake."

To her surprise he pressed a kiss to her forehead. "I must speak to the laird and find out where we can live. He often gifts warriors who marry a small plot of land."

"Do ye wish for me to accompany ye?" Grace asked sitting up and reaching for a robe that had also been gifted to her by Lady Ross.

"If ye wish. First we must break our fast."

They poured water from a pitcher into a basin and took turns rinsing their faces. Struan dropped a cloth into the water, rung it out, and washed himself. After he finished and turned to find his trews and tunic, Grace poured out the water, refilled the basin, and did the same.

Once they were both dressed, she sat on the bed and did her best to untangle her hair.

Struan waited patiently seeming interested in her movements. "Yer hair is quite a task," he commented.

"Not usually," Grace replied. "It is just that I did not brush it out last night." She looked up to see that he smirked.

"I am ready," Grace stood, and they walked out of the room, down a corridor, and into the great room. There were only a few people at the tables. First meal was just being served and Grace could barely wait. Her stomach growled at the aromas.

They sat at a table near the dais where the laird was. Lady Isobel was not seated with her husband, but at another table with several women.

To her surprise, Carla and her husband hurried over. The woman hugged Grace. "I am so very happy for ye. I was nae aware ye came to marry."

Grace accepted the woman's congratulations with a smile. "Will ye join us?"

The couple sat.

"Did ye find yer son?" Grace asked.

The woman nodded. "He is alive and well, living on the Isle of Lewis. Though he does nae wish to return to live here."

"I am sorry," Grace said, noticing that Struan spoke to a man next to him. By the looks of it, a keep guard.

"No need," Carla's husband said. "He has a large plot of land. A farm. We returned to gather what we can and move there instead."

"Ye are leaving Taernsby then?" Grace asked, nudging Struan. "Do ye have a house and land there?"

Struan turned to listen remaining silent as the couple explained they hoped to find someone to take their home and small plot of land, so that it would be cared for.

"I have a beautiful garden and we have several goats," the woman said. "I hate to leave them. They are pampered, ye see. In return, I have milk and delicious cheese."

The man looked to Struan. "Perhaps ye would consider the house. It is the one not too far from the guard's quarters on the edge of the village. Ye know, with the goats that wear coats in the winter."

Struan nodded. "Aye, I know the place. It is a good house." He looked at Grace. "Have ye seen it?"

Grace may have, but she rarely went outside the village. "I do nae remember it."

"Come see it," Carla urged. "Ye will need a home of yer own and what's better than not having to build one. The planting season is here, and it will be hard to find workers."

After the meal, Struan pulled Grace outside for a walk. They went to a garden with a short wall that overlooked the inlet. "It is a good house. I can ask the laird for it and the surrounding land, which includes a forest that comes to the shore."

"It sounds lovely," Grace replied. She studied him for a long moment. "How do ye feel?"

Keeping his gaze forward, he seemed to consider his reply. "I will always be honest with ye, Grace," Struan said. "I am not sure. It is as if I'm moving and doing what I need to do, but I am not feeling anything other than confusion."

"Ye have every right to feel angry, or disappointed. We should not have been together. It is more my fault than yers. I should have stayed in Taernsby."

"Nay," Struan took her by the shoulders. "Do not blame yerself. I took advantage of yer innocence. If anyone is to blame, it is me."

Grace lifted her eyes to meet his. "I am not sorry ye are my husband. Ye are so very beautiful."

"Beautiful?" He chuckled. "Do not call me that in front of others." Though it was obvious he liked the compliment. "It is ye who are beautiful and despite my always believing I did not wish to marry, I am glad that ye are my wife."

Pulling her close, Struan held her for a long while as they watched birds run along the shoreline, seeming to play a game with the waves.

STRUAN WANTED TO make the ride back to Taernsby in one day. "Are ye prepared for it?" he asked Grace.

Once they walked out of the laird's office with the gift of not only the house but surrounding lands, it was as if Struan felt lighter. His demeanor changed. He accepted hugs and handshakes from other guards while they emptied out his room and laughed at jokes directed at him.

Grace stood by the wagon they'd take, looking on as the last of the items were loaded. They were to stay at the inn in Taernsby until Carla and her husband left.

Although she looked forward to returning, Grace had yet to absorb what her life would be like.

Struan climbed onto the bench after lifting her onto the seat. He then wrapped a blanket over her already thick cloak, ensuring her hood was in place before he urged Brutus forward.

"I am very warm," Grace said, wondering if she'd overheat from all the coverings. The cold air on her face assured her she'd not.

Lads hurried over and placed heated bricks wrapped in burlap at her feet. They nodded at Struan before running back to the stables.

"Ye thought of everything," Grace said perplexed at the different way he treated her now compared to when they'd left Taernsby.

They rode at a steady speed, Struan seeming to allow Brutus to set the pace. The powerful horse didn't seem to mind pulling the wagon and stayed in the center of the road.

Several hours into the ride, Struan pulled the horse to a stop and helped her down to stretch her legs, as he put it.

They went in separate directions to relieve themselves, then upon her turning, she found he watched over her. His gaze moved from her to the surroundings while standing in a protective stance, feet apart, arms loose at his sides.

Grace frowned. "Are ye expecting us to be attacked?"

Instead of a reply, he hurried her to the wagon and lifted her to the bench. Once he climbed aboard he nodded. "I do not trust Duncan. Although he agreed to relinquish ye, something about him gave me pause. He did nae ask for anything in return."

"Ye said he'd not actually paid with coin but had made arrangements so that my father would not have to repay his debts." Grace shivered as the idea of being in danger sunk in.

"I have learned that men like him always have a motive for everything."

CHAPTER FIFTEEN

T HE ENTIRE RIDE to Taernsby, Struan kept quiet, his mind awhirl with the extreme change in his circumstances. He did not expect Gilbert Duncan to follow them, nor did he foresee any danger. He'd made the excuse to Grace to keep her attention away from him and the myriad of emotions that traveled through him.

Not only did he acquire a wife, but land as well. The life he never expected and if he were being honest, one he never wanted.

When they arrived at Taernsby, there was much to do. He'd leave most of it to Grace. They'd stay at the inn until the couple moved from the house, which they'd assured would be within a sennight.

Gavin would have to be informed. Then there was Torac and Erik. His stomach clenched at the overwhelming weight that pressed down on him.

"Look," Grace said pointing into the woods where a doe and her two fawns appeared. The animals seemed surreal with the background of the woods. The mother fed, while her offspring preferred to play. Jumping about and chasing one another while the doe kept vigil.

At Grace's raptured expression, Struan couldn't help but relax. "It is nae often that a doe has two."

"They are having a delightful time of it," Grace said. "I am glad to see it. Most of their life they will have to be cautious and wary. For this short time, they are blissfully unaware."

"I envy them," Struan said before he was able to stop himself.

Grace turned to him, a soft expression. "I have given our situation much thought. I think the best thing will be for ye to deposit me at my room and ye continue on to the guard post. I know ye do not wish to be married to be tied to a life that is the total opposite of everything ye desire."

"I have made a vow to ye," Struan replied, unsure what she actually planned. "We have become husband and wife in every way."

The lovely coloring of her cheeks sent a shiver of awareness through him, and he did his best to push it away. "Grace…"

"I do not wish to live with ye. I prefer to return to life on my own. Please."

"What about the house?" Struan wasn't sure why he argued. Was it not exactly what he wished for? To continue to be on his own. To not be tied down?

"Ye can have it. I have no need for so much."

"No," Struan said, setting his expression. "We will stay at the inn. Once the house is available. We will move there."

BY THE TIME they arrived at Taernsby, the hours of silence between them had stretched to a point he almost gave in and asked what she was thinking. But as stubborn as Grace was, he was twofold.

At the inn, they ate in silence. As soon as Grace finished

her meal, she went up to the room he'd rented for them.

The innkeeper was delighted to have someone staying there for a sennight, as he'd explained they had no other lodgers.

After checking on his horse and ensuring the animal was fed and settled at the stables, Struan went to the room and found Grace tucked under the covers, fast asleep.

He walked around the bed to peer down at her. In the moonlight she looked pale in contrast to the raven tresses that framed her face. Her long lashes fanned over the top of her cheeks, and her rosebud lips were slightly parted. His wife was breathtakingly beautiful inside and out.

She deserved so much better.

Yanking his clothes off, he lay atop the blankets, pulling his tartan over himself, and fell into a deep sleep.

The crowing of a rooster woke Struan, and he sat up, at once remembering where he was and the situation he was in.

Grace remained asleep, which suited him perfectly. He dressed in a hurry, went downstairs, and left a message for her with the innkeeper that he'd return later that day.

"I WONDERED IF ye would ever return," Gavin said by way of greeting. "I have changed the patrols of the cove. We are expanding to the southern shore."

The man stalked toward the tables in the back of the huge space. "Have ye eaten?"

Struan shook his head and went to a table where only a pair of other guards finished their meal.

"I have something to tell ye," Struan said. "First of all, the laird does nae wish for any guards to travel north. He plans to send twenty new guards to exchange with those here."

Gavin nodded as Alpena brought their food.

The woman gave him a quizzical look. "Ye look different. What happened?"

"I am annoyed," Struan said. "Long travel."

"No. Something else. Ye are always annoyed." Thankfully the woman let the subject drop and walked away.

Struan ate, realizing he was very hungry. Once he ate half of what he'd placed on his plate, he let out a long sigh. "I am married."

When Gavin choked on his food and began coughing, Struan waited for the man to get his breath. "I did not plan it. But the woman, Grace, she was to be given away to a man she did nae care for."

"Is that not always the case with arranged marriages?" Gavin said finally finding his voice. "What were ye thinking?"

Struan shook his head. "Not sure."

"Do ye care for the lass, at least?" Gavin asked pinning him with an annoyed look. "She is a sweet woman, with no one to look after her. If ye do not want her, that would be a shame."

"I will never mistreat her."

"Is that reason enough to marry her?" Gavin waved away whatever Struan was about to reply.

"What are yer plans now?"

"The laird gave me the McCleary's house and land surrounding it. I suppose I will be living there."

"Ye suppose?" Gavin pressed his lips together. "Flora has been worried about the lass. She hoped she'd not go through with asking for help to find her betrothed."

"I am sure Grace is with her now." Misery enveloped Struan at the thought that perhaps he'd cause more harm than good. "I am not sure what to do."

Gavin let out a sigh, seeming to calm. "Be a good husband. Do yer duty. Ye are an honorable man, Struan. I know ye will treat her well and perhaps come to care for her."

It was as if the words floated through the air and sunk into his skin, then slowly deeper until Struan absorbed the seriousness by which Gavin had made the statement.

Struan studied Gavin who did not meet his gaze. "I care for the lass. It is just that I never planned to marry."

Finally, Gavin looked at him. "Some of us wish for what ye have and it is out of reach."

It didn't take much to know who Gavin referred to. His friendship with Flora had never moved past that. To everyone it was obvious the man was madly in love with the seamstress. For whatever reason, Flora either did not feel the same, or she still grieved for her husband and child.

"Ye should talk with her," Struan said, almost smiling when Gavin's eyes rounded.

"Talk to who?" he asked, knowing very well Struan referred to Flora.

"Do ye really think how ye feel about the bonnie seamstress is not obvious? Ye have been too patient."

"She is not over her loss. If Flora has not noticed me by now, then she must not feel anything stronger than a friendship."

They finished eating in silence and then Struan remained to listen to the plans for the next few days. Several teams were to go on separate patrols, from north of Taernsby, past the cove, down to the shore, and across until almost at Erik and

Torac's territory.

Struan volunteered to go west, he hoped to see his friends and speak to them.

"Yer patrol will leave two days hence after the first teams return. Ensure ye have all ye need," Gavin instructed them.

Once everyone's questions were answered, then Gavin spoke to Struan.

"I will ride to the village with ye. I promised Alpena to pick up some items from the market in the morning."

The ride to the village was quick and upon arriving, Gavin looked toward the seamstress shop. "I am willing to bet Grace and Flora are there."

"Aye, it is probable," Struan replied. "That is where I am headed. First, however, I am going to seek a hot bath. Hopefully, my tunics are finished. The few I own are threadbare."

FLORA LOWERED TO a chair next to where Grace sat peering out the window.

"I still cannot believe what happened," she said in a reverent whisper. "Ye are married to Struan Maclean."

"Aye, and he is not happy about it. I have ruined everything with this idea to go to the keep."

Flora huffed. "I do not believe Struan would do anything against his will. Whatever happened, it was set once ye and he spent the first night together. Ye my friend should have kept from being with him."

"It would be much easier to douse the sun with a bucket of water," Grace replied.

Flora laughed.

"It is not funny."

"Oh, it is," Flora said between chuckles. "Ye and Struan have been drawn to one another since yer first meeting. It was obvious."

"What should I do?" Grace asked, her hands running across the neatly folded tunics in her lap. "Should I do my best to be a good wife, or should I release him from the vows?"

"First of all," Flora began, "ye both made vows, not just him. A promise made before God is binding Grace. Telling him that he is released, does not mean it is so. Ye will always be his wife and he yer husband."

What her friend stated was true. No matter how two people felt about one another, a vow before God was binding. "Then I will be a good wife to him."

"In time both of ye will see this is the best thing that could have happened, Two people attracted to one another who end up married makes for a wonderful marriage. Ye are fortunate."

A smile crept up and Grace smiled broadly. "I am. I am so very lucky to be Struan's wife."

Just then the door opened, and Gavin walked in. His gaze sought out Flora's. There was some sort of message between them, Grace was sure of it.

Flora looked away first. "Grace is back, so is Struan, but I imagine ye already are aware of it."

"Aye," Gavin said moving toward Grace. "I wish ye well on yer marriage."

"Thank ye," Grace said, her face warming. "Did Struan return to the village with ye?"

"Aye, he went to bathe. Plans to come here after to collect

his tunics."

"Perhaps I should go and meet him at the inn," Grace said but didn't stand when both Gavin and Flora firmly said, "No!" at the same time.

It was as if they didn't wish to be alone together.

Through narrowed eyes, first she studied Flora and then Gavin. How her friend didn't know the man was madly in love with her was something she'd not dared to ask Flora about.

Once learning about Flora's horrible loss, it was obvious she would be tentative to allow love into her life again.

The same as Struan, they feared the loss or betrayal of anyone they allowed near their heart. Instead, they did what they could to keep others at arm's length.

"Did Struan tell ye about the house?" Grace asked and almost laughed when the pair seemed to relax, glad to know she'd not leave.

"He did," Gavin said. "Ye will be staying at the inn until then. Ye should know he will be leaving two days hence for a patrol that will take about the same."

At the news, Grace felt a certain type of relief. It would be good for Struan to get away without her. Perhaps it would allow him the time to see that his life would not be altogether that different.

BY THE TIME evening came and Struan had yet to show up, even Flora was giving Grace worried looks.

"I am glad ye are here helping out," Flora said lifting the cup of warmed cider they'd had with their meal.

She'd given up waiting for Struan to eat and finally agreed to share a meal with Flora, who'd made a hearty soup, which they'd eaten with crusty bread from the bakery.

"I best go," Grace said standing. From a hook next to the door, she retrieved her cloak and wrapped it around her shoulders. "Tomorrow I plan to get my things out of the room I was living in. I am sure someone will be grateful for it."

"Will I not see ye tomorrow then?" Flora said nearing with the folded tunics. "Do nae forget yer husband's clothes."

The words sounded foreign, she still could not believe she was married to Struan. "I almost did," Grace reached for them. "I doubt it will take me long to clean out my belongings, I have very little. I will come and help ye until we move to the house."

"Good," Flora said.

Grace hesitated. "Did something occur between ye and Gavin?"

At Flora's cheeks pinkening, Grace smiled. "It is about time. The man is enamored of ye."

"I do not know what to think," Flora admitted. "He is younger than I am. What if he prefers my friendship."

At Grace's droll look, Flora giggled. "We can talk about it on the morrow. Ye best go. It is getting quite dark."

Their room at the inn was empty. Someone had started a fire, for which Grace was thankful. She placed Struan's tunics on a side table and then sat next to the hearth. There was nothing to do but think. Grace stood and paced. Glancing at the door, she wondered if perhaps she should ask downstairs if Struan had left a message. No, he hadn't. The innkeeper had greeted her upon her arrival and not said anything.

Had Struan decided to stay at the guard post?

After a long while, she yawned and decided to go to bed. She'd get up early to go and clear out the room that had been her home since coming here and then head over to work with Flora. Struan would show up eventually.

Sleep came easy once her mind settled. Sometime in the night, the sounds of Struan undressing woke her, but she didn't stir. Instead, she watched as he removed his boots, then his trews.

By the light of the fire, his muscular body was accentuated to show off every angle. Dressed only in the long tunic, he added a log to the fire and stood before it as if in thought.

Finally, he turned to the bed. Grace watched through slitted eyes as he walked closer and bent down to look at her.

She closed her eyes to make him think she was asleep. It was hard to keep from moving, especially when he carefully moved her hair away from her temple and placed a soft kiss on it.

The smell of whiskey told what he'd been up to. Obviously, he and the men had gone to the tavern for drinks. A celebration perhaps?

Struan let out a long breath, rounded the bed, and slipped between the bedding. He was cold, which made Grace shiver.

"*Shhhh*," he whispered and then he surprised her by wrapping his arm around her and pulling her against him. With a final sigh, his breathing became shallow as he quickly fell asleep.

IN THE MORNING, Grace woke to find that instead of him wrapped around her, her leg was over his and her head on his shoulder. Her arm was across his waist and Struan lay on his back, his face to hers.

How to extricate herself was a quandary. She moved her

arm, and his right hand came over cradling her.

After a few moments, Grace gave up and relaxed against her husband. The room was chilled, but he was so warm it made it hard to even consider moving. At the same time, she really had to relieve herself.

Moving ever so slowly, she managed to slip from the bed. She hurried behind the screen to use the chamber pot and then added slender slips of wood to the embers. It was much too cold to be out of the bed, Grace decided, once the fire came to life and she could add a larger log.

She shivered as she hurried back to the bed.

Upon climbing next to Struan, she lay on her side facing the fire, careful not to touch him.

"Come closer," Struan said, pulling her back until she was flush against him. "It's cold."

"It is," Grace whispered.

"I am sorry to be so late last night," he murmured in a groggy voice. "They wanted to celebrate my marriage."

"Did ye enjoy yerself?" Grace asked, genuinely interested. Hopefully, he did and was becoming accustomed to their new life.

He grunted, then replied, "Aye. I did."

"I spent the day with Flora. I think something happened between her and Gavin."

"Something bad?"

"Something romantic."

"Ah," Struan replied.

Grace wanted to roll her eyes at his lack of saying something about it. "Has he said anything to ye about her?"

"He has. They will work things out."

It was clear he would not tell her what Gavin had said, so she changed the subject. "Gavin told me ye are to go on patrol."

"Aye. I will not be gone long. Will ye be well alone?"

"Why wouldn't I be? The time away will give ye time to see that yer life will not be so different now than before."

When he pressed a kiss to her neck, just below her ear, shivers of desire traveled through her. His hand moved up from her waist to cup her breast.

"Things are very different than before," he murmured.

CHAPTER SIXTEEN

LORA FINISHED HER early morning shopping and turned the corner to head to the bakery. Coming from inside was Gavin carrying several bundles.

A fluttering in her stomach made her hesitate, but then after a fortifying breath, she crossed the path toward him.

"Are ye purchasing items for Alpena?" Flora asked eyeing the items in his arms. It looked like meat and bread.

"Nay. I was coming to see ye." Gavin met her gaze. "I thought we could break our fast together."

"I would like that very much," Flora replied, not having the heart to tell him she'd already eaten. Besides, it had only been a very light repast and she wanted to spend time with him. Since the kiss, which was probably a one-time occurrence, they'd not been alone together.

They walked toward her shop, and she noted several women giving him side glances. A pair of young lasses slowed and upon seeing him whispered and giggled.

"Ye have quite a few admirers," Flora said with a smile. "I am surprised ye had not courted anyone yet."

"I am considering it," Gavin replied with a serious expression. "I have tried to make time, but it was only now after seeing Struan settled that I realize there is more to life than just being a guard."

At his statement, it was as if a stone replaced the fluttering of just a few moments past. Flora did her best to smile, but her face did not cooperate.

"Do ye not think that moving forward is the best way for us to do what we intend to do while here?" he asked.

They'd often had serious conversations about all kinds of topics, so his question was not surprising to her.

"That is true. What purpose would we have to remain stagnant and not enjoy our life," Flora replied.

They arrived at the shop, and he waited while she unlocked the door.

Once inside, he followed her to the back of the shop to her small kitchen. In the tight space, she had to stand with her back to a table in order for him to place his purchases of thinly sliced ham, cheese, and bread on the sideboard.

He turned to her, and Flora felt as if she wanted to cry. He was so very handsome, so perfect. The flecks of gold in his brown eyes had always drawn her to look into them. Now she could only think that it was but a matter of time before they would not have any more moments like this.

"I will warm water for tea," she said turning to the stove.

When Gavin took her by the shoulders and turned her to him, she gasped. "What is it?"

"I want to court ye. I have tried to be patient, to give ye time. But I need to know." Gavin's breath fanned her face, and she could smell that he'd eaten something sweet. Her lips almost curved at knowing he'd probably had one of the baker's sweet tarts.

She was without words, for whatever reason nothing came to mind other than how much she wanted to touch him, to be closer to him.

On impulse, she lifted her hand, wrapped her fingers around the back of his neck, and pulled him down.

Their mouths crashed with a hunger that came from months and months of closeness but not daring to move past friendship.

Gavin kissed her with all the passion he'd held in check all these long months. His tongue pushed past her lips. His arms wrapped around her body, as he pulled her against him.

The feel of his body was something she could not describe. Not since her last husband had she allowed this. But the guilt she expected didn't come. Instead, it was a warmth that enveloped her. As if from the beyond, he hugged her too.

This man was to be hers, Flora had no doubt. Gavin had been so patient, coming to see her regularly. Bringing her gifts and sharing meals while they spoke of their days. After so long as friends, they knew each other so well.

When his hands slid up her sides, she was instantly aware of how long she'd desired him. He cupped her face and lifted it up to his. "Are ye crying? Ye are not ready?"

It was then she realized tears had flowed down her cheeks. "I am crying," Flora admitted with a sniff. "They are happy tears."

She reached up and caressed his jawline. "I am so very ready for ye, Gavin. I believe I love ye."

A wide grin split his face and he hugged her, lifting her off her feet as they whirled in a circle.

"Thank God," Gavin exclaimed. "Should we eat?" He placed her back on her feet.

"No," Flora said taking his hand and pulling him to her

bedroom. "We will not eat until later. Much later."

THE RAIN AND chilly wind seemed to seep through Struan's clothing directly into his bones. He grunted in annoyance at seeing a hill ahead. Once atop, the wind would be relentless.

"Head north," he called out to his men. "We will ask for shelter at the guard post near Welland."

The men gladly agreed and within an hour the post came into view.

At once, several men on horseback rode toward them, the guards ever on patrol to ensure the safety of the area.

Torac lifted a hand in greeting at recognizing him and rode closer. "What brings ye out on such a day?" his friend asked.

"The weather was not as bad when we left," Struan grumbled.

They arrived at the post and the horses were quickly taken to the stables, while the men hurried inside to the long room that had a large fire in the hearth. The aroma of a hearty stew filled the air.

Auley, the cook, looked up and nodded in acknowledgement. "Leave it to men to arrive just as a meal is about to be served."

The regiment at the Welland post was only about twenty, most of them familiar to Struan as he worked there for a time. The men greeted one another, making room at the table for him and the four who accompanied him.

Soon everyone was telling stories of days past while sharing a delicious meal.

Struan sat with Erik and Torac, who asked about the ships that had come to the cove.

"They have not returned, so we are moving our patrols out in case they decide to try a different place. Ye should keep yer eye on the coastline in case they decide to come ashore from here," Struan informed them.

"We are," Torac said. "Did ye see the laird?"

Struan told them about the laird's plan to bring men to transfer with those wishing to return to the keep.

"Aye, I heard the same," Erik replied. "The bairn was born. A lad." His face became bright with pride. "Named him Gregor Allan."

"Strong name," Struan said reaching over and patting Erik's shoulder. He turned to Torac. "And ye?"

Torac lifted one shoulder. "Not yet soon. I hope the bairn waits longer. I am not ready."

They laughed. Both looked at him when he cleared his throat.

"I am married." Struan watched as his companion's eyes rounded and mouths fell open.

"Not true," Torac finally said. "Ye are trying to get me to spit out my ale."

"It is," Struan said. "Her name is Grace. She is the most beautiful woman I have ever known."

"Grace?" Erik said, his eyes narrowing. "Grace. Does she have hair as black as a raven?"

It was Struan's turn to be surprised. "Aye. How do ye know her?"

"Ah, aye, I remember her," Torac said. "From the shipwreck. Bonnie lass. Every warrior was trying to help her. She came from the water, barely clothed, light night rail plastered to her body. She looked like a siren."

"That is my wife," Struan said with gritted teeth, not at all liking that others had seen more of her than was appropriate.

"Ye married that beauty? What did ye do? Kidnap her and drag her to a vicar?" Erik said while chuckling.

"Was she conscious during the wedding ceremony?" Torac asked fighting to keep a straight face.

Struan kept a flat expression although his chest expanded with pride at the men finding it hard to believe such a beauty married him. "She wished to marry me. I agreed."

"Only a fool would not," Erik said. "I am glad to hear it."

Both congratulated him although Torac kept giving him questioning looks. "How do ye feel about it? I know ye never wished to marry."

"I am becoming adjusted to the idea of it," Struan replied honestly.

The fact that he kept wondering what Grace did and if she was safe and warm, was new. Never before had someone invaded his thoughts as much as the woman back at Taernsby.

When Erik and Torac's lips curved Struan turned to look behind wondering what they found amusing. He turned to look at them. "What are ye smiling about?"

"Ye are in love," Torac said and let out a bark of laughter. "A miracle."

He did not argue, instead growled out something about them acting like gossiping women. But at his face heating, he considered that perhaps they were right.

LATER THAT NIGHT as he settled onto the slender cot and pulled his tartan over his body, his thoughts went to Grace, sleeping alone at the inn.

There was no good reason for being out on patrol when the weather would keep any attackers away until late spring.

In the morning they would return to Taernsby.

Once his mind was made up, he relaxed and thought about the fact that the following night he would be sleeping against his wife's perfect body.

Torac was right. He'd never felt about anyone the way he felt about Grace.

He was in love.

EPILOGUE

GRACE STRADDLED STRUAN, hands on both sides of his head as she lifted and lowered onto his thick hard staff.

His face was taut, lips parted as he held back waiting for her to find release. With a curve to her lips, she leaned down and took his mouth with hers while moving faster, taking him deeper before lifting.

"Ye have me bewitched," Struan growled taking her by the hips to speed the tempo. She gasped and then moaned as a climax threatened.

Then to her delight, he rolled her over onto her back, lifted her legs over his shoulders, and drove into her with hard fast thrusts until she screamed out in release.

A delicious heat burst from her center and into every inch of her body. "Struan!" she called out when he continued the drives as she found herself climbing again.

Suddenly all went dark, and she was floating, the only sounds were Struan's grunts of pleasure before he fell over her.

"Grace." His voice permeated the darkness and Grace fought to open her eyes.

"Grace." This time he patted her face. "Can ye hear me?"

"Aye. But I do not want to do more than remain here in this delightful place. Ye inside, the heat of yer body covering me."

They'd been inside their new home for days. And fortunately a heavy rain had fallen for days as well, making it impossible to travel.

Grace had never been so thankful for it.

"Ye are beautiful," Struan said, and she opened her eyes to find him studying her with a deep furrow between his brows.

"Are ye annoyed about it?" she asked pushing a lock of his hair from his forehead. "That ye find me pretty?"

"No," Struan said, suddenly very still. "I love ye, Grace."

Her breath caught, manifesting in a sharp intake of breath. "Ye do?"

"Aye. I think from the moment ye wanted to sell yerself to me."

Her cheeks went warm. "That was an unfortunate moment. I am so mortified by it."

"Do not be. I found ye to be brave." He pressed a kiss to her forehead. "Ye are a fighter."

"I love ye, Struan. I think since…"

He studied her. "Since when?"

"Since that day I measured ye for a tunic. I was so taken by ye, I could barely think."

Rolling to his side, he pulled her against his side. "I am so thankful that ye forced me from my stubborn vow to never marry. Ye are the best thing I ever did." He hesitated and softly added, "I trust ye, Grace."

Tears sprung to her eyes. "I will never betray ye, Struan. Understand it. Believe it. I am and always will be only yers."

When he let out a long breath, it was as if he'd been holding it his entire life. His lips curved.

"I am sorry to say, ye are stuck with this warrior for the

rest of yer life as well."

Grace giggled. "I am a fortunate woman then."

When he rolled to face her, they remained like that for a long while. Each of them still not believing their good fortune in finding one another.

A Note to Readers

Let's get to know one another,

Sign up for my newsletter and get a free Clan Ross story!

Newsletter Link: https://bit.ly/3vSEbYY

I sent out my newsletter monthly which includes book news, giveaways and sneak peeks!

About the Author

Enticing. Engaging. Romance.

USA Today Bestselling Author Hildie McQueen writes strong brooding alphas who meet their match in feisty brave heroines. If you like stories with a mixture of passion, drama, and humor, you will love Hildie's storytelling where love wins every single time!

A fan of all things pink, Paris, and four-legged creatures, Hildie resides in eastern Georgia, USA, with her super-hero husband Kurt and three little yappy dogs.

Visit her website at www.hildiemcqueen.com.

Manufactured by Amazon.ca
Bolton, ON

34101642R00101